INTO THE SHADOWLANDS

TIFFANY PUTENIS

Edited by
TARA JAZDZEWSKI, SEAMUS KING, & EBONY
NORWOOD-BROWN

Copyright © 2021 by Tiffany Putenis

All rights reserved.

No part of this book may be reproduced in any form or by any electronic or mechanical means, including information storage and retrieval systems, without written permission from the author, except for the use of brief quotations in a book review.

ISBN: 978-1-955373-03-6

Cover artist: Ruxandra Tudorica

CONTENTS

To my amazing children, whose friendship inspired Roarke and Gedran's bond.

Thank you for making me a mom. I love you.

SHADOWLANDS
CAHIR
MIRROR LAKE
AGUISTIN
THE DUCHY OF
AMADAN

"Under a red sun, the strongest of men will face the
    Demon Lord.
Driven by what is just and right,
only he can bring these shadowed lands back into the
    light."

— CAEREA, GODDESS OF JUSTICE

D uke Grainne paced his study, bristling with impatience. The demon lord was late, and the duchy's future hung in the balance. The sky faded from azure into a misty crimson blur painted with burgundy clouds as the sun went down, and shadows overtook the landscape beyond his windows. The duke gazed out of the window, running his fingers through his shoulder length black hair. His manservant scurried around the room, hurriedly building a fire in the massive gray stone fireplace that dominated the space while Grainne tapped his fingers restlessly against his leg. The beleaguered manservant brushed a thin strand of graying hair out of his face and finished arranging the wood. He lit the fire, bowed before the duke, and exited the room. Grainne rubbed the tips of his fingers together, his gray eyes focused on the larger pieces of wood, and mumbled to himself as the fire blazed to life, flames licking the timbers.

Grainne paced away from the fireplace and wandered around the room for a few moments, mindlessly shifting and adjusting the various trinkets that were on display. He straightened a bust of his great-grandfather, then knocked a spider's web loose from the corner of a painting commissioned in a prior century. Frustrated with Trahern's tardiness and beside himself with worry, he walked back to the fireplace and leaned against the wall, casually wiping his hand across his brow as he stared into the fire with a marked intensity. His anxiety grew exponentially as every second ticked by. The mahogany and brass mantle clock ticked loudly in the near silence of the chamber. Minutes passed and he slowly lost his bravado, shrinking into himself until he was hunched and cowering before the fireplace.

The corners of the room seemed to darken and the flames in the fireplace turned a deeper shade of red as shadows began to coalesce just inside the door. They twisted into a figure, appearing almost human before becoming more substantial, until the face of Demon Lord Trahern became visible, his curling ram's horns glowing atop his head, wreathed in flame. Trahern's skin appeared burnt, stretched taut against the sharp bones of his face, giving him a skeletal appearance. Grainne shrank back as Trahern approached him, fear draining the color from his face. The descriptions of him that Grainne received did little to lessen the terror of his actual presence.

"D-demon Lord, you... you honor me with your presence," Grainne said tremulously, drawing a shaking breath. His palms began to sweat. "I hope that... that we can find a way to live in... in peace."

"Peace? What peace?" Trahern's voice sounded hard, like the ice that forms on the polar lakes far to the north, and cut through Grainne, as sharp as the edge of a newly made hunting knife.

"We... We don't need to be at war, you and me. Surely we can work together to... to accomplish whatever needs to be done. I can be a great ally to you, we have many -"

"Silence." Trahern's tone demanded total obedience, and Grainne immediately closed his mouth, lest great harm come to him and his people. "I will never be at peace as long as men have the ability to wield great magic."

"Wh-what?"

"There is a prophecy about me, Grainne, that the oracles say will be fulfilled by a human male wielding great strength in the magical arts. My father cursed the Shadowlands by disobeying the covenant he made with the Gods. As the Gods cast him from the mortal realm, a prophecy was spoken by Caerea, the flaxen-haired Goddess of Justice. I must conquer all of the lands surrounding the Shadowlands to protect myself. I can either conquer you or subjugate you, Grainne. You have a choice."

Grainne nodded, his head spinning. *I don't have the strength to defeat Trahern on my own,* he thought. *Our society has been peaceful for generations, and the militia's training has focused more on breaking up bar fights and marching in parades than on actual warfare.*

A treaty appeared before him, suspended in the air by an invisible hand. The letters glowed like burning embers on the parchment. The intense glow burned his eyes. He read it once, then again. He remembered his lessons about Briomhar, now known only as the Shadowlands.

I, the undersigned, pledge to provide no shelter to the man with the greatest magical ability in each generation. After a testing, which shall occur every twenty years, the victor shall be sent into the Shadowlands by a portal, wherein he will forfeit his human belongings and titles. Once in the Shadowlands, he will be claimed by Demon Lord Trahern, never to return to the Duchy of Amadan.

In return for this tribute, Demon Lord Trahern will make no attempts to conquer the Duchy of Amadan and will leave its citizens free to live their lives. Any assault on the Shadowlands, or attempted rescue of a tribute will void this contract and result in an immediate assault on the Duchy of Amadan.

    In signing this contract, Duke Grainne of the Duchy of Amadan acknowledges that he and his progeny will be bound in perpetuity by these terms.

The blood rushed from Grainne's face, and his head spun. *Could I really sacrifice someone to keep the rest of the duchy safe? I suppose I could,* he thought. *But we would have to explain it to my subjects in a way that made it seem non-threatening. We would have to honor the sacrifices as heroes.* He looked at Trahern levelly.

"You want me to... to sacrifice each generation's most powerful magic wielder to you. You want me to send one... one of my subjects into the Shadowlands, where you will take possession of him in order to protect yourself. In return... You... you will leave my duchy free? We need not worry, as long as this happens?" He tried to steel his tremulous voice, desperate to hide his nervousness.

"Yes, Grainne. As long as you send him to me, regardless of what may happen to him, I will spare you and your pitiful little duchy. But, should you fail to do so.... You will all suffer. I will make you watch as your loved ones are ripped apart, their bones fed to my wyrmlings after their flesh is charred over demon fire." With a flick of Trahern's wrist, a pen made of bone and sinew appeared in his blood-tinged skeletal hand. "Make your choice."

Grainne's heart raced as he eyed the pen, considering all of the possible outcomes. Hesitantly, he reached for the pen, trying not to think of what, or who, it had been made from. He took it, then gasped in shock and pain. As he grasped it, it latched onto his hand, drawing his blood into itself. He signed the document, using his own lifeblood as iron-scented ink. Blood dripped from his hand where the pen bit him, and he felt the leaden weight of the blood-bound treaty settle onto his shoulders.

CHAPTER TWO

Roarke

Roarke sprang up in his bed in shock as he awoke from the dream. His hands fisted in the blankets until his knuckles went white from the strength of his grip. He closed his eyes as he released his hold on the blankets; the recurring dreams about Duke Grainne had been getting worse as the ceremony approached. He sighed, rubbing his hand where the pen would have latched into his skin. A shiver ran down his spine. He still felt the pain from the bite of the pen on his hand lingering from his dream; the lack of a mark surprised him. He shook his head and rubbed his eyes, still heavy with sleep. The rough cloth of his shirt, drenched with sweat, clung to the muscles of his chest and arms. He took a deep breath and exhaled slowly, attempting to clear his head of the superstition and fear that lingered from the dream.

"Father Llughe, patron of knowledge and strength, give me the courage to make it through today. Give me the wisdom to convince Gedran to put family before pride. Let

"

me keep the only family member I have left," he whispered, praying to the god of knowledge to assuage his fear. He felt desperate, terrified, and hoped that prayer to Father Llughe would help him. He straightened in his bed and stretched, attempting to loosen the knots in his back and shoulders.

"It was just a dream," he said out loud. "It was just a dream."

He repeated it several times, as he had every morning over the past several weeks. The words had become a mantra to help him move on from the terrible dreams that plagued him in advance of the competition. He shook his head, his sleep-tousled bronze hair falling into his verdant green eyes before he brushed it back and tucked the strands behind his ears. Pale, watery sunlight filtered through the windows of the cottage as birdsong floated in on the breeze. A chill hung in the early spring air, and the sprinkling of rain that happened overnight while he slept had left a damp sheen over the grasses and plants in the yard, which were just beginning to show the promise of new life.

Roarke thought through his dream as he undressed and wiped the sweat from his body with water and cloth from the pitcher on the dresser. *The smell that clung to the room once Trahern appeared... it reeked of sulphur, like cooked eggs gone rancid after days of being left in the sun. It turned my stomach. I wonder how Duke Grainne could stand it,* he thought. *And that pen... What was it made of? Gods, it looked like it was pulled from someone's hand. I can still feel where it latched onto him.* He rubbed his hand again, then pulled on his plain linen shirt, green woolen jerkin, and the dark brown breeches he favored.

I really don't want to do this, he thought. *It doesn't seem fair that someone should have to sacrifice themselves to the Shadowlands. None of us volunteered for this. Why did Duke Grainne think it was right to sacrifice one of us every generation?*

Throughout the duchy, the citizens rejoiced at the traditions that surrounded the testing. Roarke or Gedran, facing the perils of the tests and the potential of being the sacrificed, didn't feel the excitement of the other townsfolk. Those rejoicing were not part of the testing, or those who did not have family being tested. Testing only occurred once a generation and only included men who had shown magical abilities. Many families had no one being tested, and they reveled in the pomp of the ceremony. Those participating in the testing were kept separate from the spectators, unable to participate in the festivities or enjoy the food and drink offered by the numerous wandering merchants. The crowds traveled from all corners of the duchy to enjoy the magical displays and the ample food and wine that would be made available for the crowd's enjoyment.

Roarke didn't fear the testing itself; he feared that his older brother would win. He knew his magical limits and didn't expect to last much beyond the first few rounds, just as he knew the skill that Gedran possessed and the practice that got him there. Many regarded Gedran as the strongest practitioner of magic to have been born in at least two hundred years. Betting occurred in the days leading up to the testing, and high praise had been heaped on Gedran by the portal master and other teachers and the bettors favored him. They expected him to win in under five rounds. Roarke fretted, picking at his fingernails as he contemplated the testing and the possibility of losing his brother to the Shadowlands. While each man sent into the Shadowlands became a hero of the duchy, Roarke had no desire to be a hero, nor did he want to see his brother become a martyr. Gedran, on the other hand, took great pride in being the best in anything he tried and wanted nothing more than to be considered a hero.

Roarke walked into the main room of the cottage and found Gedran seated at the rough-hewn wood table, a bowl of thick porridge in front of him. Another bowl sat before the empty chair at the table, steam rising from the top. Roarke sat down facing his brother, and began to eat.

"Thank you for making breakfast," Roarke said. The porridge felt smooth and creamy on his tongue, with just the right amount of butter.

Gedran grunted in response, his mouth full. They ate in companionable silence; only the noise of spoons scraping against pottery bowls accompanied them.

"Gedran," he said thoughtfully, "have you ever thought about purposely not performing well during the testing?"

"Why would I do that?" Gedran's face scrunched in disgust.

"Do you really want to go to the Shadowlands?"

"Does it matter? I'm the best, and I deserve to win."

"Why is winning what matters most to you?" A tear leaked from the corner of Roarke's eye and he wiped it away impatiently.

"I'll be a hero." Gedran's focus stayed on his porridge, but irritation filled his voice.

"That's not what I mean, Ged, and you know it. Ma and Da wouldn't want you to do this."

"I will be honoring their legacy by becoming a hero to the duchy. I'll become a legend."

"And you'll be dead." Roarke's voice broke and he hastily looked away to compose himself.

"We don't know that." Gedran glared at Roarke, deep furrows forming between his eyebrows.

Roarke sighed, realizing that it was pointless to argue with his brother. Gedran would never debase himself by allowing anyone to think that he possessed less skill than he did. He held too much pride in his magical abilities. He dropped the subject, continuing to eat his porridge mindlessly, a deep sense of foreboding filling him with every bite.

He collected both of the bowls from the table after he

finished and placed them in the sink. *I'll wash them later, after we get back from the duke's stronghold,* he thought. He paused before walking over to the door, adjusting the cuff of his boot and wiping the last tears from his face.

Gedran tossed his cloak over his shoulders and grabbed Roarke's from the peg by the door. He handed it to him, opening the door while Roarke wrapped the soft wool around his shoulders. He fastened the ivy leaf clasp, touching it gently. Their mother had sewn the clasp to his cloak just before her death several years ago. As the door shut behind them, Roarke felt as though the door to his old life had slammed shut, too.

The walk to Aguistin, the small village near their home in Amadan, went quickly, short and uneventful. The scent of fresh bread wafted from the bakery, and Elyse, the baker's daughter, stood in front of the shop, hanging a sign that listed the items being baked that day. She waved at Gedran as they passed, her dark hair gleaming in the sunlight, and he winked back at her. The sound of her giggle followed them as they crossed the street. The village green, ringed by several houses and the general store, sat empty, save for Duke Laigi's portal master and the one other young man old enough to be tested with their generation. The portal master spoke quietly to the young man standing beside him, barely able to be heard over the flock of geese sunning itself on one side of the green. The families and local nobility who planned to attend had left in the days leading up to the testing, traveling by foot or horse to Laigi's stronghold. As Roarke and Gedran arrived, the portal master waved his hands dramatically in greeting.

"Yes, our last two. Greetings," the portal master said, his voice ringing out across the green. He nodded to them as they crossed into the manicured lawn. He whispered, his quiet words overcome by the sounds of crickets and birdsong that echoed through the square in the quiet morning. He cast the spell that would take them to the stronghold. A swirling oval of indigo appeared, spiraling outward from a dense black center point. It stretched and morphed into a gate large enough to walk through. On the other side, the stronghold stood, its golden stone facade glimmering faintly in the sunlight. The testing awaited them.

CHAPTER THREE

The men walked through the portal together, followed closely by the portal master, and exited onto the stone steps outside of the stronghold where a crowd gathered to watch the testing. Hawkers sold all manner of treats to the crowd; everywhere, people consumed hand pies filled with the last of the pumpkin from the stronghold's storerooms, washing them down with mugs filled with the dregs of the mulled wine from the winter solstice celebrations a few months before. A cheer rang out from the crowd as the newcomers joined the line of competitors at the top of the steps. It appeared that Roarke and Gedran were the last to arrive, bringing the number of men being tested to thirteen.

Duke Liagi appeared on a balcony three stories above the steps, and the portal master suddenly disappeared, reappearing beside his master on the balcony. He flicked his hand toward the Duke's throat and Liagi's magically amplified voice boomed over the courtyard.

"Citizens of Amadan. My dearest family, friends, and

subjects. Today is a day of celebration! Today, we honor the legacy of my most esteemed ancestor, Duke Grainne, who protected our duchy from the conquest of Demon Lord Trahern. He dared do what no other leader could, brokering peace with the Demon Lord through a treaty that prevents Trahern from attacking us. It is this treaty and its promise that bring us together today. These brave, strong men before you have all displayed magical talents that have grown as they have come of age, and they are here to be tested. They are here with hopes of becoming the hero who saves us from the Demon Lord once again."

Roarke shivered as Liagi spoke, his heart sinking further with every word as he considered the history of the duchy. One of the men standing on these steps would soon be sent to certain death in the Shadowlands. He had the unsettling feeling that it would be Gedran, and began to brace himself for the emotional turmoil that would follow.

How would I react? He wondered. *What would my instinct be?* Prior to the death of their parents, Roarke, who had never been the strongest student of magic, had trained extensively in the arts of war, becoming a master swordsman. He dreamed of one day conquering the Shadowlands and ending the Demon Lord who ruled there, effectively ending the need to sacrifice someone to protect the duchy. That ended when their parents died. Roarke and Gedran could no longer afford to study, and their focus shifted to maintaining their family's farm and flock. It chafed at Gedran, who longed to learn even more magic to increase his already formidable strength. He borrowed every book he could find and peppered the portal master with questions whenever he came through the village, determined to learn as much as he could without a formal education. Roarke devoured every book he could get his hands on when he wasn't working in the fields and practiced his combat skills on the village green against the other boys when they weren't in their lessons.

Would I fight, Roarke wondered, *if they tried to take my brother away?* A horn blasted from the balcony, startling Roarke from his ponderings. The portal master appeared in front of the men again.

"For these tests, you must pay complete attention to the spell I weave. Each spell must be completed by each of you. Anyone who cannot complete the spell will be eliminated, until only one competitor remains. Any injuries sustained during the testing will be handled by the healers. Does anyone have any questions?" The portal master looked at the line of men, all of whom nodded their understanding. "Let us begin."

The portal master wove the first spell, a small orb of arcane energy that glowed a faint purple in the air, and the men followed suit. One by one, the arcane orbs appeared over their outstretched hands, hovering and giving off small crackles of energy. When each man successfully completed the spell, the portal master applauded. Duke Laigi pronounced that all of the competitors would move forward to the next round from his balcony perch high above them.

The second spell was slightly more difficult. Above the portal master's hand, a ring of frost appeared; it floated, rotating slowly. The men attempted the spell, and one by one, the rings of frost appeared over outstretched hands. Two of the men, from a coastal village to the north, lost control of their spells. One of them, darker skinned from his time at the docks, screamed as his hand turned blue, frost appearing at his fingertips before spreading further. The other man lost his concentration as the gentleman beside him cradled the badly frostbitten hand. His ring of frost fell to the ground, shattering into a puff of snow. The crowd quieted as the frostbitten man howled in pain. As the Duke pronounced which men would move forward, the injured competitor walked from the terrace. A healer met him, carrying a basin of lukewarm water, leading him to the side of the terrace to begin the necessary first aid to heal his hand. He shrieked again as she dipped his hand into the lukewarm water to help it thaw.

"With that, we have our first two eliminations," Duke Laigi shouted from the balcony as a cacophony of cheers echoed from the crowd.

The portal master cleared his throat, gaining the full attention of the crowd and Laigi. As he cast the third spell, a pair of golden rings hovered over his outstretched palm, linking together and glowing, Roarke began to breathe heavily. The strain of trying to link the rings in his mind became too much for him. The golden rings shivered above his hand, their forms twisting as he tried to push them together. Roarke felt a trickle of blood run from his nose and lost concentration. The rings abruptly disappeared. Unable to complete the spell, he turned away and sat down alongside the other eliminated men. Roarke wiped the blood from his face and leaned against the stone wall at the edge of the terrace. His head pounded, but he continued to watch the others. Gedran outperformed everyone else, adding a third ring and linking it to the other two.

Spell number four eliminated three more men. Orbs of water the size of melons wavered in the sunlight before each of the remaining contestants, and Gedran began to show off, rotating his orb on its axis and changing the color of the water on each rotation. The crowd cheered at his antics, and he stood proudly, no strain visible on his face from his efforts. Duke Laigi preened on the balcony, clearly pleased by the crowd's reaction. The duke picked up a goblet of wine and raised it to Gedran, and the crowd went wild once more as Laigi acknowledged their favorite competitor.

The fifth spell, a swirling purple oval that resembled the start of a portal, allowed the caster to see minute details at a great distance. Another competitor failed as his portal exploded in a burst of purple confetti. Only Gedran and one other man remained. They cast spell after spell, forming balls of flame and clouds of water vapor that shielded them from view. As they cast a wall of flame, the other man's restraint failed him and his wall exploded in a shower of sparks. He fell to the ground, screaming in agony as thousands of tiny flames licked at his skin. The healers rushed to him, carrying him from the terrace.

Only Gedran remained. He stood on a dais in the center of the courtyard, hidden behind a wall of shimmering blue flame. He strutted forward, walking through the wall unscathed, and grinned at the crowd, a cloak of woven water wrapped around his broad shoulders to protect him from the flames. His bronze hair gleamed in the light from the sun and the fire as the portal master walked over to him, applauding. He lifted his arms in triumph and let the woven water spell go, causing a cresting wave behind him.

A cheer went out from the crowd as the duke stood and raised his glass.

"Ladies and gentlemen! My esteemed guests! May I present to you our victor," Duke Laigi said, his voice filled with excitement.

Gedran bowed, his eyes gleaming with pride. He turned toward Duke Laigi and raised his hand in a salute before turning to wave at the crowd. Reality hit Roarke as he watched his brother celebrate. The world seemed to slow. He couldn't breathe, and his eyes wouldn't focus. He heard nothing other than the pounding of his heart. Gedran beamed as the portal master handed him the spoils of his victory: an oilskin of water, a pack containing bread, meat, and cheese, and a heavy cloak. The portal master began to circle his hands as he opened the portal to the Shadowlands, which glowed deep blood red and swirling black, showing nothing to the audience of what could await on the other side.

Duke Laigi's chronicler, a diminutive man with thinning hair and a weasley smile, wrote Gedran's name onto the scroll of victors, to be celebrated as the duchy's champion, and he waved to the audience as he walked to the portal. Roarke tried to scream, his voice caught in his throat as his mind chanted "NO" over and over again. Gedran turned to look over his shoulder as he neared the portal, and he gave Roarke a soft smile. Tears of terror rolled down Roarke's cheeks, his face twisted with emotion. He ran forward, desperate to drag his brother away from the portal, but one of the guards caught him by the waist and pulled him backwards.

Gedran's smile turned to a pained grimace as he watched his brother struggling to get to him and sobbing hysterically; he looked genuinely shaken by Roarke's reaction as he turned back to the portal. Shock and terror crossed his face as fear for his life set in.

He stopped short of the portal, and Roarke screamed in agony. Gedran turned and tried to run to him, but the portal master stepped between them.

"I'll be ok, Roarke. It's going to be ok," Gedran shouted as the portal master pushed him toward the portal. Gedran crossed through it, and a roaring cheer went up again. Roarke collapsed as the world around him went dark.

He heard... humming? Roarke's senses winked back into existence. The faint humming to his left drew his attention as he opened his eyes. The sunlight shone brightly in his face, and the memories of the morning rushed back, twisting his face in agony again. The ancient face of the portal master hovered over him.

"Hush, hush," the portal master said, his voice pitched barely above a whisper. "Hush, hush. You made quite a scene at the end of the ceremony. Duke Laigi is pleased, very pleased. The audience loved seeing you so overcome at the loss of your brother after his victory. They especially loved seeing Gedran try to run to you before he went through the portal. Without a doubt, this will go down in one of the histories that are scattered throughout the royal library. The Duke's minstrel is already working on a new song."

"Where am I?" Roarke asked, his voice hoarse with the emotions clogging his throat. He tried to sit up, but the world spun around him. "What happened?"

"Still in the courtyard. You were only out for a few minutes, but most of the crowd dispersed quickly. Only a few spectators remain." The portal master squinted, surveying Roarke's face. "It is time for me to take you home. You are the only competitor who is still here. Do you think you can stand?"

He stood, offering Roarke his hand. Roarke accepted the help and stood, his legs shaking with the effort. He steadied himself with a hand on the portal master's shoulder for a moment, before nodding that he was ready to go. The portal master cast the portal back to Aguistin, then gently patted Roarke on the shoulder, attempting to console him. Roarke walked through the portal, his head down. As he entered the village green, he stopped and looked around with pain-filled eyes.

I remember the day all of the village boys played catch in the middle of the green. Gedran threw the ball to me, and I missed it. It went rolling into the road by the blacksmith's forges, and he stopped working to throw it back to me. I tossed it as hard as I could at Gedran. When he caught it, he waved his hand around. I could tell he was surprised by how hard I had thrown the ball to him. I must have been five, maybe six years old? I remember the day he started looking at Elyse, the baker's daughter, too. He picked wildflowers for her when we walked into town and brought them to her at the bakery. She blushed and stammered, and he looked so happy with himself. I wonder if they would have married if things were different. He's barely looked her way since we lost Ma and Da a few months later. Our lives completely changed. He shook his head, trying to clear the scenes of happier times from his mind.

We have so many memories here. How can I walk the same streets we've always walked together if Gedran isn't here?

He stood still in the center of the green, the afternoon sunlight on his skin. Tears poured down his cheeks as he mourned Gedran.

Eislyn

In the manor house on the far corner of the square, a curtain twitched in an upper-floor window. Eislyn quickly hid herself from sight, her mind racing. Her eyes, the color of golden honey, widened as she realized the outcome of the ceremony. She absentmindedly pushed a strand of unruly mahogany hair behind her ear. Gedran hadn't come home, and Roarke seemed lost without him. She gasped, tears beginning to fall as she watched him cry, carefully hiding herself from view. She grew up watching Roarke and Gedran from afar, spending her entire childhood longing to be part of their shenanigans as they played on the green. Seeing Roarke without Gedran felt wrong. The absence of Gedran from Roarke's return worried her.

Gedran must have been the victor, she thought. *Roarke won't let him sacrifice himself so easily. He has to be planning something.* She watched him walk from the green, knowing that something big and exciting loomed on the horizon. She desperately wanted to be a part of it.

ROARKE

Roarke collapsed into his chair beside the fire as soon as he walked into the cottage. The ashes of the morning's fire sat in the cold hearth, but he made no move to start a new one. His thoughts lay heavily on his mind. He stared at the hearthstones pensively and considered the options that lay before him.

I should go after him, he thought. *Da had maps of every territory near us. Nobody has traveled to the Shadowlands and survived, but I know he had old maps, from before the treaty... We must have one of the Shadowlands, too.*

He stood and raked his hand through his hair, then began rifling through the shelves in the main room of the cottage. His father loved maps and had collected many of them, purchasing them from passing peddlers whenever he could. He often told Roarke that studying the maps let him experience the world outside of Aguistin, where he had lived and farmed his entire life. Despite never traveling further than Mirror Lake, his father's passion for studying the maps proved to be contagious. Roarke studied them throughout his childhood, imagining the adventures he would have one day and telling his father all about his dreams of becoming a great explorer.

Things were so much simpler when I was little, he thought. *I never worried about the reality of exploring, only dreamed of the glory of seeing places no one had been in centuries.*

He collected one of the large stacks of maps from a high shelf where they sat, leaning between a book of poetry and the pottery crock his mother had liked to use for proofing bread dough when she was baking. He scattered the maps across the floor of the cottage and sat down heavily, shuffling them as he searched for the ones he needed.

He located the map of Grainne separately, sitting on the rough wooden shelf by the door where his father kept it. He had looked at it a few days prior to the testing, trying to determine how long the ride between Cahir and Auguistin would be. Gedran reminded him after a few minutes that they wouldn't be riding; the portal master was responsible for transporting all of the competitors.

Most of his favorite memories involved his father and these maps. The first time he had seen the map of Grainne, he sat on his father's lap as he marked the location of the farm. They talked about the farm and village, and his father showed Roarke where they lived in relation to Aguistin, the duke, and the river. The creases showed signs of wear from the countless times it had been folded and refolded over the years as they studied it to prepare for hunting and fishing trips. He gently unfolded the map once more, his fingers grazing the mark his father had made over the location of the farm. He smiled, and a chuckle escaped his lips as he remembered Gedran falling into the river during a fishing trip. He still remembered the screams and the sound of the splash as his brother fell head first into the water, fishing pole in hand.

Roarke blinked rapidly, returning to the present from his reverie, and flattened the map on the floor, careful to avoid ripping the worn creases. He stood and began pulling the other maps down from the shelf. He rifled through them, searching for a map of the Shadowlands.

If I leave early enough tomorrow and ride hard... It could work. I would have to get into the Shadowlands without being noticed, but I could track Gedran and attempt to save him if I can make it in. Nobody has ever traveled there and lived to tell the tale, so I don't have much to go on. Roarke located an ancient-looking map without a title that showed a large portion of land to the east that was labeled as Amadan. He suspected that this might be the Shadowlands; he knew they lay to the west of Amadan. Lining the two maps up on the table, he began to plot his course, reviewing the topographical landscape drawn onto the maps to determine where he would find sufficient shelter.

A thought popped into his head, and he stood and walked to the bookshelf. *It must be around here somewhere,* he thought as he searched. *I remember a book on the Shadowlands being here when I was little.*

He ran his fingers along the spines of the books, searching for the strange markings he half-remembered from his child-hood. He located the volume, bound in deep brown leather that was stamped with symbols from a language he didn't recognize, and pulled it from the shelf.

"This is it," he said. He cracked the spine of the book and began flipping through its pages, searching for pertinent information. "Not much is known about the Shadowlands, as safe passage is not guaranteed as part of the treaty. It is understood that Demon Lord Trahern has taken magical precautions to confuse and repel any humans who cross over into his territory. Based on the very limited knowledge that has been passed down through the generations following the treaty, it is likely that these precautions are hazardous and potentially deadly in and of themselves." He cringed at the dry, scholarly tone of the book.

He flipped forward several more pages before he came across something interesting.

"Stories from the time before the treaty tell of a land where ash falls from the sky like rain. The landscape is dismal, painted in shades of gray, with the exception of a lurid red sun." Roarke frowned at the description before continuing, "The Shadowlands are said to be barren, with only remnants of the plant and animal life that once existed there. Instead, the area is now filled with creatures of Trahern's own making. Nothing is known of these creatures; those who may have encountered them did not survive to tell the tale."

Roarke took out his journal and pen, then listed out what he would need to be successful. Standing, he grabbed his claymore from its mount on the wall and several daggers and belt knives from the chest near the bedroom door, then took his father's compass from his mother's jewelry box. Gedran's blanket followed along with a bedroll from the supplies their father kept in an old trunk in the bedroom; Roarke placed them on the table. He ran outside and grabbed a bow and sheath of arrows from beside the door, then filled and stacked four oilskins of water on the table. He grabbed his pack and saddlebags from their hooks, carefully filling them with the items he gathered.

Roarke walked out of the cottage and back into the pastures where the sheep grazed in the sun. He wandered through the fields, the early spring sunlight warming his skin as he checked on each of the sheep. He stopped to stroke the dense gray wool of the oldest ewe in his herd. The sheep bleated and looked up at him, then waddled away. After accounting for them all, he checked the troughs of water that they kept in various parts of the field and made sure that the pen doors were open to allow the sheep to wander back in when it was dark. He couldn't bring himself to let them out of the pastures completely; his family's livelihood depended on them. He wanted to make sure that they would be able to make it back into the shelter should a late storm hit.

They are as safe as I can make them, he thought. *It wouldn't be fair to pen them up for Gods know how long. I hope someone will see them loose and check on them.*

He walked slowly back to the cottage. The sun hung low over the horizon as the bells at the temple rang out five chimes. He shook his head, startled to realize that he lost two hours wandering the pastures. He loved to walk amongst the tall grasses and wildflowers, but time for frivolous wanderings became scarce after their parents died. Their sickness caused them to waste away before his eyes, shriveling and weakening until they could no longer care for themselves. Gedran pulled away from him then. Their once-close relationship became fraught with conflict as they both gave up their dreams in order to keep the farm afloat.

I hope I make it to him in time, he thought as he walked through the cottage door. *Ma would laugh at me for saying "I hope." She always said that hoping and wishing were fine, but that you could only reach your goals through persistence and hard work. She would tell me to pray to the Gods for success and wisdom, and I would listen. I'll definitely need that persistence now. Father Bel, patron of success and life, please let me save Gedran. Grant me success in my endeavor, as Father Llughe grants me knowledge and courage to go on.*

The air developed a chill as the sun began to set. Roarke busied himself by pulling logs from the small pile of wood just outside the cottage door and arranged them in the fireplace. Unable to light it magically, as Gedran would have, he used the flint and steel he kept in a tin box on the mantle. He struck it sharply, sparking the small piece of tinder and tossing it into the artfully stacked logs. He fanned the flames, blowing on them until the logs began to catch.

The logs crackled as they burned, and the relaxing sound comforted Roarke. He watched the flames dance amongst the kindling, leaning back against the soft, high-backed armchair that his father favored. Reaching to the table beside him, he grabbed his journal. He chewed the nib of the pen, considering, then dipped it into the inkwell and began to write. He poured out his fears, confusion, and plans onto the page, finding relief in the catharsis of writing.

Roarke wiped the ink from the nib of the pen and set it down on the table. He sanded the ink to help it harden, then blew lightly on the page to remove the excess before closing the journal and placing it into his pack. The last quilt his mother sewed lay across the back of the chair, and he pulled it down, leaning forward and wrapping it around his shoulders. He remembered watching her cut the fabric and piece it together, bit by bit, whenever she had fabric to spare. He cuddled into the blanket and watched the fire burn, willing himself to relax.

I'll ride out first thing in the morning, he thought as he stared at the flames, letting them hypnotize him. *I should really get some rest now. Who knows when I'll be able to sleep in a bed again.* He stayed in the chair for a while longer, letting the heat from the fire soak into him, warming him to his bones. He felt himself starting to doze as the flames worked their magic, relaxing him to the point of sleep. He stood and carefully folded the quilt, laying it across the back of the chair. Relaxed and emotionally exhausted, he wandered into the bedroom and fell into his bed.

Eislyn

Across town, Eislyn sat in her window, a book on the history of Amadan cracked open on her lap. The beeswax candles burned low in their brass holders on the ledge beside her. She skimmed through the pages, searching for any mention of the testing ceremony and the fate of the victors.

The treaty itself is vague regarding the testing ceremony's victors, stating only that they are forfeit to Trahern's machinations, she read. *The prophecy states that the strongest of men will defeat Trahern. It seems unlikely that Trahern would leave them alive.*

Eislyn frowned, a deep furrow forming between her delicate eyebrows. She pictured Roarke's stricken face in her mind, the grief and loss painted plainly across his normally joyful features, and her heart ached as she remembered the only other time she had seen him look that way.

The villagers gathered on the green in the early morning light. The spring air felt cool on my skin as I stood beside my parents, watching as the bishop led Roarke and Gedran to stand beside the twin coffins. Gedran looked stoic, determined to show no emotion or weakness, but Roarke... his face twisted in pain. It made my heart hurt to watch him. After the bishop finished the sermon, Roarke and Gedran walked over to stand with the villagers for the rest of the burial. They recognized Father from the times he purchased wool from them, and they came to stand by us. Roarke stood beside me, and I took his hand and squeezed it, offering whatever comfort I could. Mother saw me and flicked my ear with the tip of her finger, a silent signal of her disapproval, but I kept holding his hand until the burial was over.

Eislyn sighed and pressed her palms against her eyes, trying to stifle the tears the memory brought out. The book lay forgotten in her lap. She relived the memory of holding Roarke's hand in hers; his large hand had enveloped her own small one, warm despite the chill in the air. She hoped to do it again one day. *He must be planning something,* she thought. *The Roarke my brothers talked about, the one they sparred with during lessons, would never let his brother go without a fight.* She sighed again, then picked up the book and began to skim through the pages again as she watched the road outside from the corner of her eye.

If he leaves, I'm going, too.

CHAPTER FIVE

GEDRAN

Gedran fell to his hands and knees as he exited the portal. The rocks and sand scraped against his palms as the portal snapped closed behind him, twanging like an over-plucked guitar string. Panic gripped him. The image of Roarke's face, twisted with terror and heartbreak, weighed heavily on his mind as he realized his mistake. Sitting heavily onto a partially sunken boulder covered in a film of sand, he tried to catch his breath; his chest tightened and his heart raced. He stood. Disoriented by the red-tinged light that surrounded him, Gedran spun in a circle, eyes wide in shock. A strange mist hung in the sky, diffusing the sun's red light. Ash fell from the sky like the first flurries of snow, leaving a thin coat of film on everything it touched. The rocky ground and dead tree trunks, painted in a monotonous red-tinged gray palette by the strange sun, made the landscape around him appear otherworldly. The unnatural silence hung heavily in the air, echoing louder than a scream. He scrutinized the area around him, devoid of living plant life or any signs of animals. The hairs on the back of his neck stood on end as he surveyed the unnaturally barren landscape.

Nothing, Gedran thought. *There is absolutely nothing here.*

He breathed deeply, choking as the ashes that filled the air clogged his throat. Gedran hacked and coughed, expelling the ash, then pulled the collar of his shirt over his nose and breathed carefully. A sharp, metallic tang hit his taste buds as soon as he dared to breathe through his mouth again. His stomach heaved and he vomited what little breakfast remained in his system. He shuddered in fear as he rinsed his mouth with some of the water from his pack, anxiety rising at the strange feeling the surrounding area gave him. Few trees and plants could grow here; the lack of plantlife created the illusion that he could see for miles in any direction. The air felt dense and the stagnant smell of rotting flesh permeated the air.

This is so much worse than I could have ever imagined, he thought. *There is absolutely nothing heroic about being stranded in a desert.* Dread filled him, and his heart pounded as the sound of his pulse rang in his ears. He didn't know how to make a portal, and had never considered trying it before. Each duchy was only allowed one portal master per generation, specially chosen by the acting portal master. He traveled to Elothien, across the Great Salt Sea from Amadan, where he trained in portal magic and received his rank from the Magister's Enclave.

I wonder who the portal master will choose, he thought. *Being able to create a portal would be useful right now. Maybe I should give it a try.* He stood straighter and dusted the ash from his shirt.

No better time than now, I guess. I have to get out of here. A portal is my only chance. He focused his mind, picturing the grassy pastures where the sheep grazed just up the hill from the cottage where he had spent his entire life. The grassy knolls behind the cottage's whitewashed fence became clearer in his mind, and he could smell the fresh scent of the grass and the subtle, earthy scent of sheep dung. A sudden pang of homesickness punched into him.

I wish I had listened to Roarke. Being a hero isn't worth my life. He pushed all of his hopes for the future into the image in his head. Squinting, he mimicked the hand gestures the portal master made earlier that day. An oval swirl of indigo began to radiate outward from a deep black centerpoint, and his heart soared.

A strange popping sound from the portal brought him back to reality. He jumped as vivid red sparks began to appear around the edges of the portal, shooting out like the fireworks they saw on the village green at the summer solstice. The spell collapsed inward, and the following explosion threw him back to slam against a boulder twenty feet behind him. Stars exploded in his vision. He collapsed beside the boulder that he landed against, his head spinning from the collision.

Gods damn it, he thought, feeling his stores of magic draining. Something prevented his magic from working properly; it seemed to be siphoning from him. He pushed into a sitting position. *I wonder what is causing these issues with my magic,* he thought as he struggled to his feet. *There is something about this place that makes it feel... different, somehow.* He began to walk, angling himself toward the deep red sun hanging in the ash-filled sky of the Shadowlands. He adjusted the pack on his shoulders as he walked, and pulled his cloak more closely around himself despite the heat. He comforted himself with the memory of his mother working at her loom, weaving the cloth that had become this cloak. He could almost feel her hugging him through the fabric.

The heavy silence increased his anxiety. *I need to find somewhere safe to sleep,* he thought. *Being in the open overnight is a death wish.* He trudged along, occasionally glancing up at the sky to determine his course as he headed westward. The toe of Gedran's boot caught a rock, half-buried by the ash and dust that coated the barren gray landscape. He flew forward, stumbling and skidding. The gritty dust and rocks scraped against his palms and forearms, reopening the barely-clotted scabs from his earlier fall, and blood began flowing down his leg from a deep gash in his right knee. Leaning back and sitting down heavily, he checked the damage on his knee before tearing off a small strip of his shirt to stem the bleeding. He tied the torn strip of cloth around his knee, then stood carefully and began to walk again. He tried to ignore the pain in his leg, desperate to find shelter. He knew that it wouldn't be safe to travel after the sun went down. The legends about the creatures that Trahern let roam the Shadowlands by night had been used for centuries to deter children from unruly behavior. Childhood nightmares of wyrmlings and gorm, their claws and teeth dripping with blood, flickered through his head. He tried to gauge the position of the sun behind the mist. One spot, about four fingers-width above the horizon, appeared slightly brighter than the rest. Using that as his guide, he guessed that he had just over two hours to find shelter.

Time passed slowly, and Gedran's limp became more pronounced as he trudged onward. His stomach growled, and he reached into his pack, removing a strip of dried meat. He chewed on it as he walked, though it did little to assuage his hunger. The gash in his knee ached; the strips of cloth dug into his skin, scraping against the newly formed scabs and making it difficult for him to move. In the distance, against the dismal gray hills, an outcropping of rocks stood, silhouetted by the setting sun.

Pulling the waterskin from his pack, Gedran sipped the water as he studied the rock formation, trying to figure out what it resembled as he moved toward it. *It looks like the hat the bishop wears at the solstice celebrations,* he thought. *I need to get to those rocks before darkness falls. That's the closest thing to shelter I've seen since I came through the portal.*

He picked up speed, drawing on every ounce of strength left in his body to make it to the shelter the conical rock formation provided. The red sky darkened into the deep maroon of congealed blood, and Gedran broke into a desperate run. His head swam and blood flowed freely down his leg again as the fresh scabs ripped open. He approached the rocks and squeezed into a small opening, bracing himself against the narrow corner at the back of the triangular chasm. Wedged in tightly between two leaning rocks on the edge of the conical formation, he crouched, leaning his back against the roughened stone. A preternatural screech echoed through the rocky valley, followed by maniacal laughter and screams of anguish. Gedran shuddered, curling into a fetal position where he sat. The air around him echoed with continuous screams of pain and terror and the unhinged laughter. He gripped his hands into his thick hair, rocking back and forth, the sides of his shoulders scraping against the rough stone through his shirt, desperate to soothe himself against the panic that gripped him.

CHAPTER SIX

Roarke

Roarke gathered the food he would need for his journey from the dry storage by the dim light of a tallow candle. He grabbed a large chunk of pungent aged cheese and several large strips of dried beef seasoned with salt and cracked peppercorns, putting them into his pack, then grabbed a few pieces of fresh fruit and a pair of potatoes. He arranged the food carefully in one of the saddlebags, placing the potatoes at the bottom to prevent them from bruising the delicate flesh of the apples and figs. He secured the ties on the saddlebags, then went out to the hitching post and saddled his father's mare. Once the saddle, saddlebags, and pack were secured to her, he strode back inside to make sure he hadn't missed anything. He buckled on his sword belt and sheathed his claymore, then placed a pair of short swords into a sheath on his back. He strapped a mace and two short swords behind his saddle, then tied on his dagger and belt knives. His Da's old bow and a quiver full of arrows followed, strapped across his back.

Roarke took one last walk through the cottage, engrossed in the memories of his family. He remembered his parents, seated in the armchairs by the fire one evening, not long after Gedran began to excel in magic.

"Look, Riordan!" His mother shouted, as Gedran lit the fire in the hearth with an incantation. Pride filled her voice. "He did it! Gedran lit the fire with the incantation the portal master taught him!"

Da leapt from his chair and picked up Gedran, spinning him around in circles. Ma clapped and clapped, and I walked over to the hearth to study the flames. I remember trying to figure out how they were different from the flames Da lit every day with his flint and steel, but they looked exactly the same. Later, Gedran would try to teach me the incantation, but I wasn't able to light the flame. Even though I wasn't as strong as Gedran was with magic, Ma and Da were proud of me, too.

His heart wept at the realization that he may never see this place again. He steeled himself against the pain as he looked back through the door of the only home he had known in his life. He closed the door and mounted the horse, looking back over his shoulder one more time. He spurred the mare to a canter, heading toward the road to the village.

He rode toward the edge of Aguistin's village green in the pre-dawn light, the horse's hooves echoing in the silence. Dim firelight glowed from the forges at the blacksmith's shop on the outskirts of the village. The smith raised a hand to him, clearly curious about Roarke's presence on the road so early in the morning.

"Good morning, Roarke," the smith said as Roarke rode past him. He eyed the various knives on Roarke's belt and the bow slung across his back. "Going hunting?"

"Yes, sir," Roarke said. "I'm hoping to get a deer so that I can sell the extra meat to trade for more feed. The herd grew this spring."

The smith nodded. "Good luck to you, then."

He waved, then wrapped his cloak more tightly around himself in the early morning chill. He whispered quietly to the horse, patting her mane, and turned down the left fork of the main road before urging the horse to a gallop that matched the pounding of his heart. He focused on the road, picturing the map in his head as they traveled, determined to beat the odds and rescue his brother. Distracted by his thoughts and the conversation with the smith, he never noticed the gleam of candlelight in the upper window of the old stone manor house diagonally across the green.

Eislyn

Eislyn extinguished the candle. She watched Roarke from behind the pale ivory of her curtains as he rode along the main road, noting the direction he was heading. When he rode out of sight, she rushed to her wardrobe and pulled out the breeches and shirts she hid from her father. She threw them into her saddlebags alongside her extra pair of boots and piled the saddlebags next to a bedroll and pillow. She rushed to dress in a pair of tan breeches and a gray linen shirt. She pulled the breeches up, but they slid down her hips until she wrapped a thin leather thong around her waist. She pulled the leather tight and secured it with a hefty knot. With her breeches secure, she bent, pulling on her soft burnished leather boots.

Thanks for sneaking me your old clothes, Ryan, she thought. *I'm sure you never expected me to use them to run off after one of the local farm boys.* She giggled. Glancing around the room, she packed up her small satchel of healing herbs and poultices, carefully wedging it into the saddlebags between her clothes and an extra pair of boots. The small leaden vials, filled with her carefully mixed herbal remedies, broke easily. She couldn't risk them breaking as she rode.

She flung her bow across her back and checked her quiver to ensure it held, then threw her cloak around her shoulders and snuck down the servant's stairs at the back of the manor before slipping out the kitchen door and rushing to the stables. She hastily saddled her horse and tossed her saddlebags over his back before climbing into the saddle.

"Shh," she said under her breath, patting the gelding's neck. "We have to be very quiet until we get out of town."

Eislyn rode out of the yard, keeping the gelding to a slow walk, careful to avoid the hard packed ground of the road in an effort to stay unnoticed. She turned and rode out of town, following the hoofprints of Roarke's horse in the growing light.

ROARKE

Roarke rode through the day without stopping, avoiding the roads so that nobody else would notice him. He knew that the smith would mention his departure to someone, and he refused to let anyone stop him.

This is definitely treason, he thought as he rode through the trees. *If I'm caught, the punishment will be steep.* He needed to make it to the copse of trees marked on his map before sundown. The trees became thicker along the sides of the road, blocking it from view. In the distance, he heard the laughter of a group of travelers. He moved deeper into the trees, increasing the distance between himself and the road. The late afternoon sunlight filtered through the newly budding leaves, casting dancing shadows on the forest floor.

He approached the area he had marked on the map the

day before. A forest had grown up around the copse he was looking for, and he found himself following a meandering path between the trees before he dismounted. He took a moment to stretch before striding to stand along the bank of the river. A rustle in the brush of the forest revealed itself to be a rabbit, and Roarke forced himself to be still before quickly drawing an arrow and shooting. The arrow flew past the rabbit, spooking it. He nocked his bow and waited, utterly still. Breath held, he studied the underbrush, watching carefully for signs of an approaching animal. A rustling sound came from the underbrush ahead of him, and Roarke tensed, adjusting his arrow on the bowstring and preparing to loose. As the quail wandered forward, he released the arrow. It struck the bird through the flank, felling it, and Roarke sprang forward.

Thank you, Mother Flidaira, he thought, a quick prayer of thanks to the Goddess of the hunt.

He hastily built a small fire and plucked the feathers from the quail. He saved the longest one to use as a quill, should his pen break, and busied himself cooking the bird. When the skin of the quail sizzled from the fire and turned golden brown, he removed it from the heat and doused the flames so that the light and smoke wouldn't be seen. Crouching beside the now-extinguished fire, he ate the quail, savoring the taste of the smoke-seasoned meat and picking the bones clean. He wiped the grease from his fingers onto his breeches and buried the bones and the remains of the fire before covering the area with leaves, twigs, and branches to hide its existence.

Roarke pulled out his belt knife and the feather he had saved earlier, slicing into the calamus to shape it into a proper nib for writing. Pleased with his work, he sat on the stump of a long-dead tree and grabbed his journal, flipping to the next empty page. Squinting in the dim light of the fire, he began to write. He poured his thoughts about Trahern and his weapons training onto the pages, a deep crease forming between his eyebrows as he contemplated the danger that lay ahead. When he felt satisfied with his entry, he lightly sanded the ink and placed the journal into his pack. He pulled the bedroll and Gedran's blanket and pillow from his saddlebags. He unrolled the bedroll and sat down, arranging the pillow and blanket. Wrapping himself in his heavy cloak, Roarke curled up on the bedroll beside his tethered horse, resting his head against Gedran's pillow. His brother's scent, a mixture of sandalwood and linseed oil, still clung lightly to the fabric of the pillowcase, and the familiar scent twisted in his gut. Intense homesickness and sadness for his brother filled him, and he choked back tears as he rolled onto his back. He lay still, staring up at the leaves of the forest's canopy as they swayed in the light breeze. He let their graceful movements hypnotize him until he dropped into a deep sleep.

CHAPTER SEVEN

Eislyn

Eislyn slid off her horse and stroked his mane. She crouched, studying the fresh hoofprints in the mud. The early morning dew lingered on the forest floor, dampening the ground enough to leave distinct hoofprints in the mud of the narrow path that wound through the trees near the river.

Father Bel, thank you for blessing me with success this day, she thought as she studied the tracks. *I will do everything I can to help him, I swear it.* She noticed a pile of leaves and twigs strewn over the scattered ashes of a campfire and knew that she had found Roarke's camp. He camped only ten minutes from where she had stopped for the night, nestled into soft grass buried beneath the low-hanging branches of an ash tree. The fresh hoofprints helped her get an idea of Roarke's direction.

Eislyn remounted her horse and trotted along the path through the trees, watching for signs of where Roarke went after starting down this path. Her whole body vibrated in excitement as she rode. She contemplated the things she had heard about the Shadowlands and the creatures that made it their home.

We know so little about the Shadowlands, she thought, *even though we have a treaty with their leader. I wish more of Grainne's writings existed from the time before and directly after he signed the treaty. What happened during Trahern's conquests that led him to sign the treaty and sacrifice his own citizens, rather than risk a war? Signing that treaty must have been difficult. I can't imagine agreeing to sacrifice some of my own people, even if it protected the others. Mother always said I was meant to be a warrior, unlike Ryan and Paidrig, who preferred the easy way in life like Father. It's a pity that Father wouldn't allow me to train in hunting and tracking the way they did... Thank goodness Ryan liked to rebel and taught me how to track and use a bow.*

Eislyn's heart felt heavy as she thought of her mother; she decided not to leave a note behind when she left in the early morning light. *Mother must be beside herself with worry, now that they've noticed that I'm gone. I refuse to feel guilty for this,* Eislyn thought. *I've never been the lady they wanted me to be. I want a life like the ones I've read about my whole life. I hope they'll forgive me for running off.*

A snapping noise brought her rapidly out of her reverie. She saw a doe halt several yards away, its eyes trained on her, completely still from fear. She stilled, her breathing quiet and slow, as the doe watched her. The majestic creature broke eye contact with her and loped away. She gazed in the direction the doe ran, then noticed a scrap of fabric caught on a branch ahead of her to the left. *There,* she thought. *That's where he went.* She urged her horse forward, rushing toward the branch, and snagged the fabric from the branch.

"This looks like the fabric of Roarke's cloak. I remember Father telling me that his mother was an excellent weaver; he always went out of the way to buy fabric from her when she had some to sell. He must have gotten stuck on the branch and pulled loose," Eislyn said softly to herself. "It's still warm. He was here, not too long ago." She rode on, moving through the trees at a slow pace and watching as the sun shifted toward the west, watching for signs that he was slowing.

She dismounted a short time later to sit at the base of a massive tree and eat some of the hard biscuits and dried beef from her pack. Satiated, she removed the bowstring from her pack and restrung her bow, then nocked an arrow and leaned against the tree's trunk, her hips wedged between two gnarled roots. Satisfied that the tree provided sufficient shelter, she closed her eyes and dozed. When darkness fell, she shook herself awake. She snacked on more of the dried beef and drank deeply from the largest of her waterskins before continuing to creep quietly along the road using the light of the moon as her guide. She led her gelding by the reins as a deep chill settled into her bones from the unseasonably cold night air.

She heard a soft crackling sound in the night, off to the right of the road. The faint flare from the licking flames of a well-built fire appeared in the distance, partially hidden by a boulder deep in the trees. She shushed her horse and patted his nose before the two trod through the forest, heading toward the warm light. She tethered the horse on the opposite side of the camp from Roarke's horse and crept toward the fire. Roarke slept with his back to the fire, facing away from her as she approached. She heard the soft sound of his snoring over the crackling flames and chuckled quietly. His horse nickered a quiet greeting to Eislyn as she approached, and she shushed him with a gentle stroke of his muzzle.

She eased herself down by the fire and rubbed her hands together. She shifted closer to the flames, and the heat slowly brought feeling back into her extremities. As her fingers thawed and her body warmed enough to move comfortably again, she decided to look around the camp, her gaze flitting between Roarke and his various supplies. She found his pack on a large rock near the fire, not far from where he lay sleeping. Sliding the sheaf of maps from the pack, she noticed the small, leatherbound book just below them. She studied the maps for a few moments, trying to determine the route that Roarke was taking before giving into her curiosity regarding the book. Plucking it from his pack, she settled closer to the fire and began to read.

I wish I had someone to keep me company on this journey. I keep finding myself chatting with the horse. I'd do almost anything to feel less alone. I can't help but feel ridiculous as I tell him all of the things I am thinking and feeling. Even as I wish for someone to keep me company, I know that I could never put anyone I care about through this journey. I could never ask someone I cared for to risk their life for me as I am choosing to risk mine for Gedran. As each moment passes, I am more worried that I won't make it to Gedran while he lives. I know that I must not give up hope, but he has been in the Shadow-lands for three full days now, and no one knows what happens to the chosen one after they are sent through the portal. I suppose I should be proud of Gedran for meeting his fate and going through the portal willingly, since the other chosen men have had to be pushed through the portal due to their fear. Not Gedran; he was never afraid of anything, even if it may cost him his life.

I made camp in the late afternoon today. It was a long day of riding through the forest, and worrying about Gedran is eating me alive. I could hardly keep my eyes open after the fire was made. I had to force myself to eat and write this entry, and, even now, I am struggling to stay awake to finish writing. I hope to cross the border into the Shadowlands tomorrow afternoon, early enough to find a defensible place to camp. I know from what I've read of Grainne's writings, that the portal they send the chosen man through exits close to the border between Amadan and the Shadowlands, just far enough in to be difficult for the sacrifice to find his way back into the duchy. The portal site is marked with a large, arrow-shaped stone with an ornate carving of the letter "T." Once I locate the portal site, I can begin to track Gedran. I have to save him from this fate. There must be a way to defeat Trahern without Gedran being killed.

-Roarke's travel journal.

Eislyn wiped tears from her eyes and closed the journal, tucking it back into Roarke's bag. Her heart ached at the realization of how long he had felt alone and his desperate need to save Gedran. She knew... she had *always* known that his kindness was greater than anyone realized. The memory of the day of his parents' wake floated into her mind again. She remembered the feel of his hand in hers and the heartbroken desperation in his tight grasp. She knew that she needed to help him save Gedran, even if it cost her life.

She grabbed branches and a small log and added them to the fire to keep it going through the night. She edged closer to the stoked fire and sat, her arms wrapped around her legs. She watched the flames dance amongst the kindling and prayed quietly to the Gods to help Roarke save his brother. She began to doze. The quiet crackling of the fire lulled her to rest as the flames turned kindling to coals.

CHAPTER EIGHT

GEDRAN

Gedran's breath came in short bursts from exertion. Blood coated his belt knife, but the monstrous creature still towered above him, its sinuous, scaled body slithering closer. The scrapes and scabs on his knees and palms screamed with pain as he dodged to his left. He fell to the ground beside a small boulder as the creature's scaly tail whipped toward him, missing him by inches.

A wyrmling, he thought to himself. *That was too close. I should have paid more attention to the armsmaster when Roarke and I took sword lessons. I always thought I would have my magic to protect me. I have to be quicker.*

He straightened slightly, delving his memory for the fighting stance that the armsmaster had drilled into the boys in his class. *I am, without a doubt, the biggest fool to ever exist,* he thought. *I'm sure Roarke and the armsmaster would both agree.* He spread his legs shoulder-width apart and flipped his belt knife in his hand. He tried to keep his knees bent in the casual fighting stance he had watched Roarke fall into a thousand times, but the scabbing from his fall kept him from bending too deeply. He squared his shoulders and took a deep breath. He exhaled and glanced around, checking for any other threats as the wyrmling sized him up, moving in sinuous waves back and forth. Finally, it darted toward him, its fore-claws flashing as it struck. One razor-like claw slashed his shoulder, and he screamed in agony even as he thrust the knife upward. It drove into the soft underbelly scales, and the wyrmling's momentum pushed the knife further through its flesh.

Blood spilled onto Gedran as the wyrmling collapsed onto him. He reached up, struggling to push the weight of the creature off of his torso. Grasping ribs and trying to avoid touching the monster's intestines, he pushed the putrid pile of flesh and entrails away from him and rolled onto his side. He pushed himself into a sitting position and his stomach flipped. He vomited stomach acid and the remnants of the hard bread he had scrounged from his pack earlier in the day.

Filthy and covered in gore, he stood. He needed to find water to clean himself; the scent of blood would attract every hidden predator in the area. He could feel the blood hardening on his skin and clothing, making movement difficult. Using the last of the water in his waterskin, he cleaned off his face so that he could fully open his eyes. Gedran remembered seeing a small pool not far from where he had been attacked. He headed that direction, hoping that the scent of death wouldn't attract anything else before he could clean himself off.

The closer he got to the pool, the stranger the water appeared. From a distance, it reflected the sky like Mirror Lake did, gray-red clouds moving across the surface as the wind roiled the water. Looking at it closely, the ripples in the water appeared to grow darker and thicker before snapping back to the clear water that he was accustomed to.

No other options, he thought as he stripped out of his blood-soaked clothes. He carefully dipped the sleeve of his shirt into the water, watching for any unexpected consequences. When he pulled the sleeve out of the water, it was unharmed and the bloodstains were much less visible. He washed his hands and arms, scrubbing the dried blood from them, then grabbed his shirt from the shore. He dunked it into the water, scrubbing at it with his hands and wringing it out until the water that dripped from the shirt ran clear. He laid it out on a rocky ledge beside the pool to dry, then repeated the process with his breeches before jumping into the pool.

Gooseflesh bloomed across his skin as he scrubbed his hands over his body in the frigid water, desperate to be clean. Despite having grown up on a farm, Gedran had never taken part in the slaughter. He hid in his room at slaughter time, cloistered with his spell books. He experienced no pleasure from his first kill, though he knew that Roarke would be proud of him if he knew. His only focus now was removing the wyrmling's blood from his body and finding shelter before another creature found him. He finished scrubbing his body clean and climbed from the pool. He looked closely at the gash from the wyrmling's claw; it gaped open, nearly an inch across at its widest point.

It's much worse than I thought it would be, Gedran thought. His head spun as he looked at the rent skin. The hot air contrasted sharply with the chill of the water droplets on his skin, and the blood dripping down his arm felt like fire. He sat heavily and focused inward, feeling for his stores of magic. His skin dried quickly from the heat of the red sun as he began to work the spell to heal his arm.

"Leighis mortis," he muttered, "Leighis mortis fuil, leighis en saorsa." Gedran felt the skin struggling to knit itself together; the aura that drained his magic lessened the effectiveness of the healing spell. The blood continued to flow from his wound. "Leighis mortis," he screamed, feeling the first throes of panic clutch at his throat, stealing his breath. A thick scab began to form, stopping the blood from flowing down his arm. Dizziness overtook him, and he leaned against the rock where his clothing lay drying, resting his head against the rough stone until the world stopped spinning around him. Feeling more steady, he stood carefully. Pulling on his breeches, he dressed again, determined to find shelter before darkness fell.

Gedran looked up at the sky. The fight against the wyrmling cost him hours of daylight that he needed. Travel in the darkness held risks he could not afford to take. The distorted sunlight drifted toward the horizon. At best, two hours of daylight remained before twilight would blanket the Shadowlands. He walked in the direction of the wyrmling's corpse, remembering the rocky outcropping he saw just before it attacked. Vultures screeched above his head, circling the area where the corpse rested. He shuddered at the sight of them diving from the sky and carrying steaming entrails away in their beaks.

I hope I can make it there before it starts to get dark, he thought. If he remembered correctly, it was about 300 yards between the wyrmling's corpse and the pool, and the rocks were about 180 yards past the corpse. *I can't stop for any reason. I have to keep moving.*

He picked up the pace, focusing on the horizon as he walked. A strange shrieking echoed through the desert, and Gedran jumped in terror before breaking into a run. Desperation pumped through his veins, pushing him to move further and faster with each stride. A short distance away, a pig-like snout protruded from behind a small outcropping of rocks.

"Yes, run. We will catch you in the end," the gorm muttered to itself, a cruel smile stretching across its stony, cracked face as it watched Gedran run. Satisfied that he wouldn't make it much further, it skittered away, determined to remain unseen as it traveled back to its camp.

CHAPTER NINE

Tudras ran through the red sandstone halls, its chest pumping from exertion. The pack leader of the Gorm, it had been chosen by His Mightiness to report on the prey's movements. He could not let His Mightiness down. He rounded the corner into the throne room, threw open the door, and collapsed onto its knees.

The music screeched to a halt as the caged musicians stared at it from their captive orchestra amongst the rafters. The succubi froze, their bodies pressed against one another as silence fell over the room. His Mightiness sat upon the throne, one leg thrown over the arm with graceful indolence. A scowl crossed his face and he stood. Tudras's stomach flipped as his master strode toward him, horns ablaze in fire.

"What have you found?" Demon Lord Trahern shouted as he approached his minion.

"The prey, Mightiness. The prey has been attacked by a wyrm." Tudras flinched as Trahern grabbed him by the scruff of its neck.

"What?" Trahern raged, shaking the Gorm leader. "You allowed him to be attacked?"

"No, no. Not allowed. Had no choice. The wyrm was not where it was supposed to be. The prey defeated it, but took a wound he was required to heal. We saw him clean himself in Crimson Lake. He ran away from there and we lost him. Tudras will make sure he is found, yes? Tudras will deliver him to Master."

Trahern dropped Tudras and turned away. "His stores of magic will be depleted. You cannot apprehend him now, or there will not be enough left."

Tudras said nothing, staring at Trahern and backing away slightly. *Cannot argue with His Mightiness. Tudras does not want to die,* it thought. *Tudras must live to lead the Gorm.*

"Imbecile!" Trahern shouted, backhanding Tudras across its face with his skeletally thin hand. "You could have cost us everything."

"Master, Tudras did not intend..."

"Silence!"

Tudras cowered, clutching his face where Trahern's hand struck him. A crack formed in the stony outer layer of its skin, pebbles crumbling away from its cheek. A tear of dust fell from its swollen eye. Blood-tinged sputum dripped from its snout. Trahern unlatched the whip from his belt, its steel-covered tips glowing in the red firelight.

"Pitiful creature. You will not fail me again." Trahern said, raising the whip above his head and cracking it once.

The Gorm jumped, fear creasing its stony features. "No, Mightiness. Tudras will not fail. Tudras will secure the prey and bring him to Master." It turned and shuffled away, picking up speed as it got closer to the door.

TRAHERN

Trahern watched as the hunchbacked gorm scurried away, its strange stony head dipped low in obiescence. Wrapping the whip back into a coil and hooking it back to his belt, he stalked back to his throne. The flames surrounding his horns cast dancing shadows across the faces of the succubi as he passed. They watched him carefully; he felt their eyes on him. He seated himself and snapped his fingers. The musicians resumed playing, their string instruments echoing through the hall. The succubi began to sway in time with the seductive music. Their eyes flickered to his spot on the dais, their anxiety palpable as they moved, smoothing their delicate dresses over their skin.

"You," Trahern said, gesturing to one of the nearby succubi, who pursed her mottled black lips at him, "come here." He patted his lap.

She approached him, smoothing the sheer fabric of her dress over her ample curves. Her indigo skin, almost glowing, shone through the fabric. She pasted a polite smile on her face as she approached the dais and mounted the steps.

"Yes, Master?" She whispered, her voice breathy.

"You please me," Trahern said. "Join me upon my throne."

She tucked her tail and wings tighter to her body and turned, seating herself carefully on his thigh. He smiled slightly, his lips stretching across pointed teeth, an unnerving sight even for those who regularly attended his court. The succubus looked back at him, a small measure of fear in her eyes, and his smile widened.

Yes, you should fear me, he thought. *You have seen what I am capable of. You know that I can ruin you in a single moment.* He trailed a hand down the side of her body, revelling in her shiver of pleasure and fear. *Ah... Perfect.*

"Entertain me, pet, until the Gorm return to tell me that my prey has been found."

CHAPTER TEN

ROARKE

Dawn broke in the distance, painting the sky in soft pinks and golds as it chased away the darkness. Roarke rolled onto his back and groaned before sitting up. He stretched, rolling his head from side to side to stretch out the stiffness from sleeping on the ground. He turned toward the fire, which had burned to ash as he slept, and saw her.

"What the hell," he said. He looked at the woman asleep beside the fire and shook his head. He checked the traps around the exterior of the camp; they sat in the same spots as he left them, undisturbed. Letting out a deep sigh, he walked back and stared at her again, unsure what to do.

She rolled over and mumbled quietly, caught in a place between sleeping and waking as the sky lightened. As he watched her stir, he made a snap decision. He stooped and grabbed her shoulder, shaking her awake.

"Ugh. What did I ever do to you?" she asked, trailing off into a yawn.

"Who the hell are you?" He drew his belt knife and pointed it at her.

"Roarke? You.... you really don't recognize me?" Eislyn schooled her face into an impassive mask, desperately trying to conceal her hurt. After years of casual interactions with him throughout their youth, not to mention that moment at his parents' wake, she had hoped he would remember her.

He studied her face, taking in her petite nose and pointed chin. She narrowed her eyes at him, a small crease forming between her eyebrows, and brushed a thick strand of dark hair behind her ear. The familiar gesture triggered a memory: a scrawny young girl in silks, holding his hand as he mourned. *She couldn't have been more than thirteen*, he thought.

"Eislyn."

"Yes." Amusement glittered in her eyes.

"What... Why?"

"I saw you come home without Gedran. The look on your face... He had been sent to the Shadowlands." She paused, looking deep into his eyes. "Then I saw you leave, early in the morning, sneaking through town. I knew you were planning something dangerous, and I wasn't going to miss out on a chance to be part of it." She shrugged slightly, then smiled at him. "Besides, you need me. Someone has to keep you from getting yourself killed."

"I don't need you, Eislyn. You'll just get in my way." He turned away from her, grabbing one of his saddlebags from its resting place beside the fire.

"Don't be a fool, Roarke. A blind man could have followed you through the forest."

He tossed a look at her over his shoulder and raised an eyebrow. "Oh? I find that hard to believe."

She smirked at him, then knelt and began arranging the detritus on the forest floor to hide the evidence of the fire that burned through the night. Roarke watched as she worked, humbled by the skill she displayed at masking the fire. When she finished, she stood and brushed the dirt and debris from her hands. The leaves and detritus hid the small burn area completely from view. He looked at her, his eyes wide.

"I mean it. A blind man could have followed you. I'm going with you. If you try to send me home, I'll just track you again." She crossed her arms, a crease forming between her eyebrows.

"Have you always been this stubborn? I seem to remember you being a nice, quiet girl." He paced back and forth, disturbing the areas she had just finished covering up.

"Quiet," she said, her voice trembling with mirth. "I've never been quiet. You should really spend more time with the villagers, Roarke. You don't know anything." She walked over to the mess he made. "Now stop moving around, you're messing up what I fixed." She finished hiding the signs of the camp and stood, brushing the dirt and leaves from her hands and then rubbing them on the sides of her stolen breeches.

Roarke looked her up and down as she stood, admiring the curve of her bottom. Women in Aguistin were never seen in breeches. *I wonder what Ma would think of her,* he thought to himself. *She would have been scandalized by the breeches.* He smiled, remembering the face his mother made whenever something bothered her. *She probably would have seen the appeal of being able to move freely, though. She would have appreciated the desire to help someone, too. Ma always helped anyone who needed it.* He studied Eislyn more closely, his eyes roving from the tips of her toes, clad in soft brown leather boots, up to the smooth-cheeked perfection of her face. He met her eyes, suddenly realizing she was fully aware of his gaze, and blushed bright red.

"Enjoying the view?" She winked at him, but her voice dripped with sarcasm.

"I, uh... I..." He trailed off, uncomfortable with the directness of her gaze.

"Never seen a woman in breeches before?" She smirked, then picked at a speck of dirt caught under one of her well-manicured fingernails.

"No, I haven't. It's not exactly common in Aguistin." He flushed a deeper shade of red at her scrutiny.

She shook her head, laughing, and walked to her horse. She patted his nose and murmured to him, gently stroking his mane. Hefting the saddle over his back, she secured it and climbed into the gelding. Seated astride, her posture perfect, she looked down at Roarke with a challenge in her eyes.

"Are you coming or not?"

He hurried to saddle his mare, then climbed on. Stroking the side of her neck, he clucked his tongue, and she tossed her head, shaking her red roan mane.

"There's no chance I can get you to go home? This isn't a fun ride through the forest. There's the possibility that neither of us will survive the trip through the Shadowlands," he said.

"Absolutely not. I've waited my entire life for an adventure."

She must be crazy, he thought as he stared at her. *What kind of girl wants an adventure?* He shook his head. "Let's go, then." He clucked his tongue again, digging his heels into the mare's flanks and rode away from the camp.

Eislyn trotted after him, admiring his skill with his horse as they traversed the densely treed path through the forest. She caught up as the path widened and smiled at him, flashing the small dimple that formed at the corner of her mouth. They rode side by side in companionable silence, steering their mounts through the underbrush. The soft crunch of dead leaves beneath horses' hooves accompanied them through the forest, creating a sharp counterpoint to the soaring birdsong from the heights of the trees. Roarke glanced at her from the corner of his eye, then cleared his throat.

"Can I ask you something?" He asked quietly, keeping his eyes focused on the path before them.

"Uh huh," Eislyn said, nodding as she turned to look at him.

"Why did you really come after me? We barely know each other. Other than my parents' wake, I've probably seen you 4 times in my entire life."

"I... I don't really know how to explain it," she said, a crease forming between her eyebrows as she thought about his question. "I've always felt a connection to you and Gedran. My brothers attended lessons with the armsmaster at the same time you did, and they always had stories about the two of you." She blushed, her cheeks tinting with a becoming peony pink. "They made your bond seem unbreakable, especially after you lost your parents. Ryan was upset when you stopped coming to lessons because he thought you were the only opponent worth sparring with. When you came home from the testing without him, I knew something was very wrong. I couldn't let you face whatever it was alone."

Roarke looked at her, puzzled that someone cared deeply enough about him and his brother to want to help him. They had been alone for several years, and no one in the village had offered them any type of assistance.

"Why did you never try to help us or talk to us?"

"Mother is the Duke's cousin and expects us to be separate from the other villagers because of our noble blood, and Father never stands up to her. At your parents' wake, when I held your hand... They were so angry with me after that. It was weeks before they let me go out of the manor again. They let my older brothers learn to hunt, and the armsmaster taught them to wield swords and maces with the other boys their age in the village. Me, though... I was expected to sit still, dress prettily, and apply myself to my embroidery." She grimaced.

"I can't imagine you doing embroidery."

"That's because I'm abysmal at it," she said, laughing. "I was allowed to read because Mother felt it was important for a well-born lady to be able to. I read everything I could find, especially stories of adventurers and explorers. I lived vicariously through books because I knew what was expected of me as a lady. I've waited my whole life for an opportunity like this."

"And here you are," Roarke said.

"Here I am." She smiled at him, swaying in rhythm with her horse's movements and hummed quietly to herself.

I remember this song, Roarke thought. *Ma used to sing it while she worked at the loom. I wish I could remember the name...*

"What's that you're humming?" He asked, longing to put a name to the familiar melody.

"'The Fisherman's Wife,'" she said absentmindedly as she straightened on her horse. "The cold winds blow off of the sea, the boats come to the shore, in the distance his voice calls to me, as he returns once more..." Eislyn sang quietly to him. She watched the path in the distance, and startled as the brush moved ahead of them. "Roarke. There's something up there." She pointed in the direction of the disturbance.

Her words startled him from his memories, and he leaned forward in the saddle, following her hand as she pointed toward a small copse of bushes surrounding a clearing. Eislyn sat completely still, barely breathing in an effort to make as little noise as possible as she strung her bow and slid an arrow from her sheath. Ahead of them just off the path stood the largest bear he'd ever seen. His eyes widened, and as he gasped the bear jerked its head toward them at the sound. The bear's muzzle dripped with gore, its eyes glowing a preternatural red. A moment passed as they stared at each other. Roarke held his breath, staring the bear down, trying to make himself as large and intimidating as possible. The bear charged toward him. He took a deep breath and turned, preparing to give Eislyn directions. Fear drained her face of color, her skin deathly pale, but she held her bow at the ready, an arrow nocked. He watched as she exhaled slowly and released the arrow at the bear.

The string of the bow twanged, launching the arrow toward its target. It struck the bear in the neck, lodging deeply in its flesh, but its charge didn't slow. It roared and turned toward Eislyn, sending a chill down Roarke's spine.

I have to protect her. He jumped from his mare and unsheathed his claymore, standing in front of Eislyn. She nocked another arrow and held for a moment, watching carefully as the bear continued to run. As it closed the gap between them, she loosed. The arrow struck home, hitting the bear in its eye. It stumbled, a gurgling noise came from its throat, and it fell, bleeding heavily from the wounds in its neck and head.

Roarke looked at Eislyn, unsure what to think. She caught his eye and shrugged, a wide smile flashing her dimples, then leapt from her horse to pluck the arrows from the bear's corpse.

CHAPTER ELEVEN

Sitting by the fire, Roarke watched the flames dance, his journal and quill on the ground beside him. His skin felt like ice after patrolling the outer edge of their camp in the frigid night. He rubbed his hands together, holding them before the fire. The flames hypnotized him and he lost himself in his thoughts, feeling the warmth sink into him. He flexed his fingers as feeling flowed back into his hands, then grabbed the journal and quill. Dawn broke as he finished writing in his journal, detailing his experiences finding Eislyn asleep in his camp and the fight with the bear.

Eislyn had insisted that they take watches after the bear attack, and had also insisted that she take the first watch. He acquiesced after several hours of argument while they made their camp and ate the rations she brought with her. He guessed that they had about nine days of rations remaining; they would need to start hunting soon, before they hit the Shadowlands. After Eislyn's display with the bow yesterday, he knew that they would be more than capable of providing fresh game for themselves.

If the maps are accurate, we should be just over two days from the border between Amadan and the Shadowlands, he thought. The records on the animal life beyond the border were spotty and likely unreliable; he doubted anything they found there would be edible.

He looked at Eislyn, curled onto her side and snuggled into the pile they had made of their two bedrolls. She looked like a little girl when she slept, her face smooth of the worries that weighed upon it during the day. She tucked her exposed hand between the bedrolls in her sleep, cuddling more deeply into the old quilt wrapped around her. He would have to wake her soon to give them ample time to ride and hunt before darkness fell again. He felt guilty having to wake her; sleep had eluded her in the early part of his watch. She tossed and turned for hours before her breathing evened out into the slow rise and fall of sleep.

He assuaged his guilt by stoking the fire and putting the crusty bread beside it to warm before he woke her. She jumped at his light touch on her shoulder, her hand immediately grasping the dagger she'd hidden between the bedrolls before she slept. He leapt backward to avoid being slashed.

"Eislyn! It's just me," he said, trying to keep his voice steady.

"Roarke. Gods, I am so sorry." She sat up and shook herself.

"It's fine. You're still on edge from yesterday. I don't think I thanked you for saving my life. Thank you. That bear would have killed me if you hadn't been here."

"I'm sure you'd have seen it. But you're welcome. I'm glad I was here with you."

Roarke smiled at her and held out a hand to help her stand up. She stood, brushing off the debris that accumulated on her hair and clothing from a night of sleeping under the trees. He broke the crusty bread in half and held out the slightly larger piece to her.

"Eat up. We have to get going soon so that we have time to hunt. Based on the maps, it looks like we are about two days away from the border. I don't want to rely on whatever game we'll find once we cross into the Shadowlands."

"Smart. I've never read anything about the wildlife there, but I suspect it'll be far from hospitable. I'm positive it won't be edible."

She stood to dress, and her efficiency astounded him. His experience with women left much to be desired; his only close female relative was his mother. His memories of her dressing for her day were dim, washed with gentle rays of sunlight. He pictured his mother in his mind, straightening the bodice of her gown or adjusting her sleeves, as he watched Eislyn unbraid and brush her hair before braiding it back into a thick plait nearly the size of his wrist. She finished her ministrations and bent to roll the bedrolls and blankets. He smiled at her back before turning away to put everything back into his pack.

She's beautiful. I don't know how I didn't notice, he thought. Across the fire from him, she put away her belongings in her saddlebags and fastened her bedroll to the back of her saddle. He stood and walked to his mare to pack his own saddlebags.

"Did you sleep well?"

"I suppose. Thank you for agreeing to let me take the first watch," she said. "Killing that bear wound me up, and I had a hard time relaxing."

"It was no problem," he said, grinning at her. "I was exhausted, so I didn't mind getting to sleep first. Plus, taking shifts means we can double up the bedroll."

"That was a definite benefit." Eislyn smiled back at Roarke, then busied herself covering the evidence of their camp. When she finished, she hopped into her saddle and maneuvered her horse next to Roarke's. He studied the map closely and failed to notice her approach. The gelding knickered quietly behind him, and he jumped.

"Did you have to sneak up on me?" Consternation filled his voice.

"I didn't know that Croga would do that," she said, laughing.

"Croga? Only you would name your horse 'brave,'" Roarke said.

Roarke wiped his hands on his breeches and threw himself into his mare's saddle, steadying himself with his knees. They set off at a walk, the horses' hooves crunching in the detritus that lined the forest floor. The earthy scent of pine needles and damp soil wafted on the light breeze that wound its way through the trees. The animals of the forest remained hidden as they passed, and their placid pace allowed Roarke to relax. He let his mind wander as the birds sang in the trees, embracing the moment of peace being offered to him.

Eislyn began to hum again, the same tune as before. *What had she called it?* He thought to himself. *Something about fish? I should ask her again, but I don't want her to think that I wasn't listening to her the first time.* He nodded his head in time to her musical hum, then picked up the tune himself, humming a deep counterpoint to her soprano notes. She looked at him, clearly startled that he joined in, and he smiled at her, continuing to hum. They rode on companionably, humming together and watching for game amongst the trees.

In the forest to their left, a twig snapped. Roarke whipped his head in the direction of the sound. He held his breath, staring at the doe that stood a short distance away from them, nibbling on a low-hanging leaf. He heard Eislyn slide out of her saddle, the soft soles of her boots quiet against the ground. Her body brushed softly against his leg as she passed between their horses, gently stroking Roarke's mare. She shushed the horses and peered around Roarke toward the doe. Crouching beside them, she quietly drew an arrow from the quiver angled across her back. She nocked it to her bow, drawing it back until her hand lightly brushed against her cheek. A deep breath expanded her ribcage, and she loosed the arrow on a soft twang of the bowstring as she exhaled. The arrow flew, just nicking the doe's flank before sailing wide. The doe startled, then darted away. Eislyn loosed another arrow, catching the doe high in the back flank, watching as it stumbled. A third arrow hit, sending the doe careening to the ground.

Roarke jumped from the saddle and ran to the doe. Her eyes rolled up toward him as he approached, and he sighed inwardly as he slid his belt knife from its sheath and ran it across her throat. Her eyes became glassy, and he gently slid them shut.

"That never gets easier," he said, sadness filling his voice. He sat down heavily. "I grew up on a farm, slaughtering lambs and cattle with my Da, and it still cuts through my soul every time."

Eislyn crouched beside him, wrapping an arm around his shoulders.

"That's because you were raised to respect life," she said. "Even if it's a necessary thing, you still respect the creature enough to feel its loss."

Roarke stared at her in shock.

"Wait... what... Eislyn," Roarke said. "How do you know that? We barely know each other, and you didn't know my parents at all." He looked at her, awed at her ability to understand him.

"My father spoke of your mother often; he knew her quite well and often purchased fabrics she wove. Her respect for all creatures was something that he found fascinating."

"She always talked about how important it was to treat

animals well. She wanted us to understand the importance of life for everything, not just ourselves. Gedran was never bothered by the slaughter, but I..." He paused, a thoughtful look on his face. "I always felt sad when it was time, despite knowing that it was the way of things."

"Knowing something doesn't make it easier. Your mother would be proud of your empathy," Eislyn said, her eyes locked on his. "You're a good man, Roarke."

He looked at her, searching her face for deeper understanding. He didn't understand how she understood him or why she cared so much, but he knew he was lucky that she found him.

She moved her arm slightly to rub his upper back. He leaned into her hand, exhaling a quiet sigh, and hung his head. She rubbed his back gently until he moved away. He shifted to his knees and began to skin the doe, sorrow painted across his features. As the skin came free, Eislyn gathered large, pliable leaves from the trees and placed them in a pile beside a flat rock near the base of a tree. She moved to kneel a few feet away, building a fire to roast the venison and fashioned a spit from branches and twigs. Roarke finished sectioning the meat into manageable pieces, then brought it over to her. She pulled a pack of herbs from her saddlebags, removing a sprig of rosemary and a small pouch of salt. They speared it on the spit and seasoned the meat, then sat beside the fire while the early afternoon sunlight filtered between the leaves.

The crackle of the firewood created a quiet melody as the scent of smoke and roasting meat filled the air. A light breeze rustled through the canopy above them, raising goosebumps on Eislyn's skin, despite the fire, as the flames danced merrily amongst the branches and kindling.

"Mmm," Eislyn said. "I love the scent of woodsmoke and cooking meat."

Roarke smiled at her. "The scent of flame-cooked food always reminds me of Ma and cold winter evenings. She would roast mutton over the fire for hours while we tended the flock. The scent of wood and food cooking greeted us as soon as we entered the yard."

"I used to hide in the kitchens whenever Mother wanted me to work on my embroidery. Cook kept a chair near the fire for me, and I would sit and read while they worked the spits and cooked our dinner," Eislyn said. "She would sneak me cheese pastries." She arched her back, stretching her arms above her head and turned to look at Roarke.

He stared unseeingly into the fire, lost in his thoughts. A look of deep sadness painted his face. The forest air cooled as the sun shifted toward the western sky. Eislyn turned the spit slowly and they sat side by side in companionable silence, watching the meat as it roasted. Once the meat finished cooking, they wrapped it in the leaves Eislyn gathered and separated it between their packs. With the size of the doe, they wouldn't need to hunt again for several days.

"I think we should camp here for the night," Eislyn said, her voice quiet. She watched Roarke as he startled at her words.

"I think you're right," he said. "I'm sure you're weary from hunting and preparing the doe."

"Some rest will do us both good. We can ride for a longer time tomorrow, if we need to, to make up for the few hours we lost today." Eislyn stood and crossed to her horse, unlacing her saddlebags and removing the bedroll from behind her saddle. She carried them to a clear spot beside the fire, then crossed to Roarke's horse, who nickered as she approached. She stroked the mare's flank and nuzzled her side before removing Roarke's saddlebags and bedrolls. She carried them to him and sat beside him again, searching his face for a glimpse into his mind. She saw the sadness there, and the exhaustion and pain of his journey, and knew that he needed the rest more than he would ever admit.

"Let's get the rest of the camp set up," she said. "Then we can get some rest. I'll take the first watch again."

Roarke nodded his agreement, and unrolled his bedroll. He lay it out beneath the low-hanging branches of a willow tree, then grabbed Eislyn's roll and added it to his own. Exhausted and unable to continue any further, he lay down and watched the fire until he fell asleep.

CHAPTER TWELVE

They packed everything and buried the fire before mounting their horses and riding in the direction of the Shadowlands. They neared the edge of the forest and the landscape began to change around them. A strange scent, heavy and metallic, permeated the air once they passed the outermost edge of the forest. The large trees became smaller, their leaves sparse and falling from skeletal branches. The birdsong from the forest quieted to a faint whisper in the background. They rode for another mile before the sky grew hazy and gray and the sun glowed, tinting the landscape the red of freshly spilled blood.

A shiver ran down Roarke's spine as he realized they passed the barrier into the Shadowlands. No one in hundreds of years had traveled there and survived to tell the tale. He regretted not spending more time sifting through his father's books before leaving the cottage. The collection of myths and fairy tales his father preferred contained the only real information he could find regarding the Demon Lord Trahern and the Shadowlands. He thought back to what he read before leaving, then came to an abrupt realization: Eislyn mentioned being an avid reader; she may know more about the Shadowlands.

"Eislyn," he said. "What do you know about the Shadowlands?"

"Not much," she said. "I did some research after you came home without Gedran. Beyond the traditional myths that have been handed down and the story of Duke Grainne's treaty, only a few writers have ventured into the lore surrounding Trahern and his cursed lands."

"Cursed?" Roarke's eyebrows shot toward his hairline in surprise. "What do you mean, cursed?"

"I found a book written by a scholar about 200 years ago when I was researching; he wrote extensively of the creation of the Shadowlands and Abbaddon's pact with the gods. Not much is known about the time before Abbaddon lay with Trahern's mother, Lilia, beyond the terms of his pact. He vowed before the gods to never procreate and bound the vow with his blood. By siring a cambion, he broke his pact and a great plague struck." She took a breath, shaking her head.

"The land withered and became infertile. After centuries of decay and malevolence, it became known as the Shadowlands. The scholar believed that the plague was the gods' wrath at Abbaddon's betrayal of the covenant they struck with him. The gods believed he was prevented from begetting any offspring, but Lilia's powers as a succubus proved to be strong enough to overcome the blood vow." She paused, looking at Roarke, who stared at her in silent shock. "Abbaddon and Lilia ran wild for 20 years, teaching Trahern all of the depravity they were famed for, as the land rotted around them. The Shadowlands became the desolate wasteland it is today, its people killed or reshaped into the twisted monstrosities that Abbaddon and Trahern created. When the gods finally caught up to them, Lilia had hidden Trahern away."

"She hid him from the gods?" Roarke's voice sounded incredulous. "How is it even possible to hide someone from the gods?"

"I wish I could tell you," she said. "Nobody has written any details on the subject. He began hunting magic users soon after his disappearance. Once Abbaddon was sent to the pits of hell, the gods considered their work complete. Trahern's treaty with Duke Grainne betrayed another piece of the covenant with Abbaddon, but he cannot be punished under it because he was never meant to exist." She shook her head slightly, then grabbed her water skin and took a long drink.

"So he isn't bound by the covenant that bound his father?" Roarke said, puzzlement written across his face. "That doesn't make any sense." He swung out of the saddle and off of his horse and twisted at the waist, stretching out the sore muscles in his back.

"From what I understand, because the covenant intended to prevent Abbaddon from reproducing, any offspring he could sire were not anticipated. When he broke the covenant, the Gods threw Abbaddon out of our realm and into the spirit realm." She twisted her braid absentmindedly, gazing at Roarke's stricken expression. "He is there now, sitting on the high lord's throne in the pits of hell, lording over the demons and lost souls that dwell there. That punishment satisfied the covenant, and the treaty with Grainne was signed before the Gods could force Trahern into a new covenant."

"So Grainne's treaty prevented the gods from stopping Trahern?"

"To be completely honest, I'm not sure they considered him to be much of a threat. Because his mother, Lilia, is only half-demon, it's likely that they didn't anticipate that his powers would swell to what they are." She paused, stretching in the saddle. A shiver ran down her spine and she shuddered as she surveyed the vast emptiness ahead of them. "Clearly, he takes after his father."

"I thought the gods were infallible. Isn't that how they're portrayed in the stories?"

"No one is infallible, Roarke. Not you, or me, or Gedran. Not even the gods. Their mistake cost them. From what I've read, magic is important to the gods, so losing a strong magic user every generation weakens them."

"And yet, they do nothing to stop it." His mouth hardened into a thin line. He gazed at her, his face stony and unreadable, then looked away, deep in thought. After a few moments, he said, "But there must be some way to break the curse on the Shadowlands."

"If there is, it hasn't been discovered or discussed. The only way I could see is to defeat Trahern, and even that may not be enough to reverse the damage to the land itself."

"Then we have to kill Trahern. Not just to save Gedran, but to break the curse on the Shadowlands, too." Roarke's brow furrowed with determination as he set his mind to the task.

Eislyn looked thoughtful for a moment, then straightened in her saddle and nodded at Roarke.

"This is treason, Eislyn. I am breaking a treaty and going against the duke's wishes. Are you sure you don't want to go home?" Roarke asked her.

"I'm not going anywhere. You might be crazy, and this is definitely treason, but I won't let you do this alone." She pulled her horse closer to him and reached down, touching his arm and looking into his eyes. "I'm with you."

He smiled up at her and placed his hand over hers, grasping it, then walked to his horse and climbed into the saddle. They rode on, further into the Shadowlands. The landscape began to change around them. The foliage that filled Amadan became sparse, and the spaces between the trees became wider. Dusty soil flew into the air with each hoof beat.

Screams filled the sky as the blood red sun began to set. The air chilled. *We'll need to find shelter soon*, Roarke thought. *Being in the open once night falls seems like a bad idea.* He looked at the surrounding landscape, scouting for places that could potentially serve as shelter before noticing the dark silhouette of a rocky outcropping ahead in the distance.

"Eislyn," Roarke said, his voice shaking, "we need to find somewhere safe to rest for the night. I think we should try heading toward that group of rocks ahead of us to see if it's a good option."

"Ok, let's go. I don't want to be in the open any longer than we have to be. This place..." Her voice trailed off, anxiety furrowing her brow. "It gives me a really bad feeling."

"I know. Me, too. Let's get over there and see if we can set ourselves up for the night."

They rode ahead, working their way toward the leaning rocks. As they got closer, Eislyn noticed a strange shadow in the sky directly above them.

"Roarke. What is that?" She pointed to the shadow, which moved in a slow, sinuous circle.

"I don't...." He looked up, then gasped. "Eislyn," he said, a slight tremor in his voice betraying his fear. "Get your bow ready."

She looked up and saw the wyrmlings, their long, slender bodies weaving through the air, propelled by leathery wings covered in scales. Unable to hold down her panic, she shrieked, her lungs burning from the exertion. She reached behind her for her bow, stringing it quickly, then slid an arrow from the quiver hanging from the side of her saddle.

"Deep breaths, Eislyn." Roarke's voice soothed her

slightly. He slid down from his saddle, steadying himself with a hand on his horse's flank.

She focused on her breathing as she nocked the arrow. She aimed and loosed as the first wyrmling dove toward Roarke. The arrow took the creature through its nostril, a spurt of dark blood raining down around them. The wyrmling fell heavily to the ground and she jumped from her horse, retrieving the arrow from the corpse. The other wyrmlings circled, darting forward and then withdrawing, searching for the right moment to attack.

Roarke drew his claymore, gripping the leather-wrapped hilt of the massive sword, and readied himself into an aggressive battle stance. Two more wyrmlings dove at him, and he lunged forward. He moved as though his blade was an extension of his arms, dancing and darting between the creatures as he fought them with deadly efficiency. Eislyn nocked another arrow and took aim, loosing at the remaining wyrmling that circled them. She hit it in the eye, knocking it from the sky. She whooped in delight as the creature fell, the thrill of making a nearly impossible shot filling her.

Roarke continued swinging at the wyrmlings on the ground. His pace slowed as the exhaustion began to set in. His battle against the pair of creatures dragged on. Eislyn watched as he stumbled, and one of the wyrmlings took the opening, lunging at him. Its foreclaws tore through his jerkin and into his skin, ripping a preternatural shriek from Roarke's throat. He fell to one knee, grasping his abdomen.

Eislyn roared. Heart pounding with rage and anxiety, she loosed arrow after arrow in rapid succession. She battered the wyrmlings with arrows, knocking them back with each impact until they lay prostrate on the ground. Roarke struggled to his feet, one hand pressing the wound on his abdomen. He steeled himself, reaching for his sword, and swung it, beheading the first wyrmling as Eislyn sent an arrow through the other's skull.

The wyrmlings dispatched, Roarke collapsed to his knees again. A low moan escaped him as his eyes glazed with pain. Eislyn rushed to him, pulling at the torn fabric of his tunic to check the wounds beneath it. She kept her face calm, not showing her fear as she saw the extent of the gashes left by the wyrmling's foreclaw. She helped him to his feet again and got him to his horse and into the saddle, tying him to the pommel. She walked the horses at a slow pace across the pitted ground, careful to avoid any hazards that would jostle Roarke. He moaned in the saddle as the movement of the horses shifted him into an uncomfortable position.

After an hour of picking their way around obstacles at a painstaking pace, they arrived at the strange rocks that Roarke had noticed earlier. Eislyn hastily tied the horses to a waist-high, narrow rock at the edge of the formation, then untied Roarke and helped him out of his saddle. His knees buckled as his feet hit the ground, and they fell. His full weight landed on top of her and crushed the air out from her lungs. She lay still for a moment, catching her breath. Roarke groaned, rolling off of her and struggling to his feet. She wheezed for a moment before laughing hysterically.

"I can't believe that just happened," she panted between peals of laughter.

She climbed to her feet and dusted herself off. They walked into a large covered opening between two rocks. The rough redstone opening created a small cavern with a slim band of sky visible above their heads, and they saw signs that someone else had been through recently.

"I wonder if this is where Gedran camped the night he was sent through the portal," Roarke said, his voice thoughtful. He dropped his saddlebags and pack onto the ground, then collapsed beside them, leaning back against the coarse stone wall.

"I'm not sure," Eislyn said, "Everything I've read implies that the portal the sacrifice is sent through is far enough from our borders to keep them from finding their way out of here."

"Did you look around as we rode through? Each direction looks exactly the same." He bent to pick up his journal, which had fallen out of his pack when he set it down. His face blanched as pain radiated through his abdomen. Coagulated blood glued his shirt to his skin.

"Roarke, sit down," Eislyn said. "Let me take a closer look at your wounds." She hurried to get her medicinal herbs from her belt pouch, then pulled a small assortment of twigs from one of her saddlebags and started a fire to heat some water from the large waterskin they carried with them.

Roarke eased himself to the ground, careful not to stretch his abdominal muscles as he moved. He watched as Eislyn measured herbs and placed them in the water to steep. She turned to him and peeled the rough cloth of his shirt from his skin. A mewling noise escaped Roarke's throat.

"Shh," she said. "We need to get your shirt the rest of the way off. Do you think you can help me?"

Roarke nodded, grimacing as he raised his arms slightly to help her. A low moan escaped his throat. Eislyn pulled on the shirt until it snagged on his broad shoulders, then maneuvered it off of one shoulder, then the other. She set it aside, then pulled the small pot from the flames and carried it over to where he sat. She dipped a clean cloth into the warm herbal water, then gently dabbed at the skin around the wounds. He jumped, inhaling sharply as the concoction stung the three diagonal gashes across his abdomen.

"It's ok," she said, shushing him as she continued to dab at his wounds. "I have to clean it so that I can apply a poultice to prevent infection."

"I know, but it hurts," he said, cringing at the whine in his voice. The herbs in the water burned like acid as they worked to disinfect the wounds. He looked away. *Please don't need stitches. I can't let her see me pass out from seeing a stupid needle,* he thought. *I would never live that down, especially if she told Gedran about it.*

"It'll feel better once I spread the poultice on it." She finished cleaning the wound, then dried it carefully. She studied the gouges left by the wyrmling's foreclaw.

"Roarke, I'm so sorry. The wounds have clean edges, but they're a lot deeper than I thought they were. I'm going to have to stitch them," Eislyn said, keeping her voice as calm as possible.

Roarke's face went pale at her words. He looked down at the now clean wounds that stretched across his abdomen. They gleamed, damp and bloody. He nodded his agreement and laid down on the rocky ground, his head pillowed on his saddlebags. Eislyn grabbed the small sewing kit from her pack and held the curved needle over the flames until it glowed orange, sterilizing it before threading it with the silken embroidery thread from her kit. When the needle no longer glowed from the heat of the flames, she sat beside Roarke, grasping his hand and squeezing for a moment before she carefully slid the needle through his rent flesh. His hand bit into the tender flesh of her thigh at the first penetration of the needle and he gritted his teeth against the pain.

After several stitches, his grip on her leg loosened and his hand fell limply to his side. He slid into unconsciousness from the pain.

Eislyn worked hurriedly to complete his stitches. As soon as she finished, she spread a generous coat of the poultice from her pack over the wounds and loosely covered it with clean linen. *A full wound dressing around his torso will have to wait until he regains consciousness,* she thought. *There's no way I can lift him to wrap the bandage around his back.* Physically and emotionally exhausted from the battle and treating Roarke's wounds, Eislyn lay down beside him. She pillowed her head on his shoulder, falling asleep to the reassuring rhythm of his heartbeat.

Roarke thrashed in his sleep, trapped in a torturous dream. He tossed and turned, striking Eislyn with his desperate flailing. She woke with a start as his hand hit her abdomen and rolled over as he began mumbling to himself. She rubbed the sleep from her eyes and sat up, pulling his head into her lap and softly stroking his hair. As she stroked his hair, she noticed blood seeping through his shirt above his wound. She pressed down on the bandage to help stem the flow. He groaned, turning his head and burying his face into her thigh, unable to escape the nightmare.

Gedran ran. The screams and cackles of his pursuers followed him as the strange creatures gave chase. He panted, the muscles in his legs straining as he pushed himself faster. He heard the laughter closing in behind him. Turning, he hazarded a glance over his shoulder to gauge the distance between himself and his pursuers. His foot caught in a rut in the dusty, pitted ground, and he plummeted forward, catching

himself on his hands and knees. He felt the scaly hands of his attacker grasping at his ankles, the rough skin scraping against him as they pulled him backward. He dug his fingers into the dirt, desperate to grab hold of something that would keep them from pulling him away.

No, no, no, he thought. A scream ripped from his throat. His captors' clammy, rough-skinned hands gripped his ankles, pulling them together and binding them with ropes.

They hauled him up, and one of the creatures threw him over its shoulder. They carried him toward a large rock beside a wide chasm filled with lava. Large hooks stuck out of the craggy rock face. The blood rushed to Gedran's head as the creatures flipped him upside down, stringing him up by the ankles. His head dangled several feet above the edge. The fiery lava bubbled beneath him, occasionally splashing the top of his head. The smell of burnt hair filled the air and the creatures howled and cackled.

"Trahern will peel your skin off layer by layer, yes," one of them said. Its voice sounded like the squeak of unoiled door hinges. It stood less than four feet tall, with a pig-like snout. Its skin was charred in several places, like a piece of meat left too long on the fire. "He will flay you bit by bit until nothing is left but wyrmling snacks."

Gedran flinched. He smoothed all emotion from his features while they taunted him, closing his eyes and trying to recall a happy memory from his childhood. His face hardened like stone as he focused. The creatures spoke his language, but their voices sounded strange, like they spoke through water. He refused to let them see the effect their taunts were having on him. The sound of heavy footsteps approached, and the creatures' chatter cut off abruptly. Gedran opened his eyes as Demon Lord Trahern strode toward him, wreathed in shadows and flames, the horns on his head silhouetted in the red sun. Gedran shivered as he approached, a deep, burgeoning fear blooming in the pit of his stomach.

"My sacrifice. So good to see that the Duke of Amadan continues to honor the treaty," he said, his voice hard and cold, like a shallow

pool during the depths of winter. Trahern sniffed the air. "You smell of magic and fear. Good."

Trahern strode closer, dragging a talon-shaped fingernail down the back of Gedran's shirt, rending the thin linen fabric in two. He shoved his hand onto Gedran's skin, delving into his stores of magic. His touch seared into Gedran's skin, and he screamed in agony. His flesh charred and withered as Trahern's magic ripped through him, intruding on his magical stores as he poked and prodded them to determine their depths.

"Go ahead, scream. No one who hears you will try to save you, foolish mortal," Trahern said. "None of my creations would dare to cross me." He gestured to the strange pig-like captors that secured Gedran to the hooks.

He pulled the whip from his belt, snapping it into the air. As it came loose and unfurled, a pulsating orange glow encompassed its tip. Trahern's mouth split into a wide smile, revealing rows of razor-like teeth, and cracked the whip. The air around it changed, shimmering and pulsing with power. He cracked the whip again, this time grazing Gedran's skin.

Gedran gasped as the whip struck him, feeling his stores of magic begin to deplete at the touch of the thong against his skin. The whip cracked again, and he howled in agony. His skin began to tear, blood dripping down his shoulders and to the lava below, and the whip continued to flay him, freeing him of his skin and his magic. Each lash elicited a new scream, and soon the echoes of pain and terror became the soundtrack of the surrounding landscape.

Roarke woke with a start, his brother's screams still echoing in his ears. The pounding of his heart echoed in his head as deep, ragged breaths wracked his body. He forced himself to slow his breathing, determined to relieve the pressure in his chest and help the panic subside. His hands fisted in the fabric of his shirt as the fear receded and he became more aware of his surroundings. He felt Eislyn's fingers in his hair, gently stroking and soothing him. Her touch grounded him.

I wonder how long she's been doing this, he thought to himself as the muscles in his back and neck relaxed at her gentle ministrations. He reached his hand up and gently stroked her arm before rolling onto his side, his head still pillowed in her lap. He quickly fell into a deep, dreamless sleep. Exhausted, Eislyn gently moved his head from her lap and onto the saddlebags. Darkness still blanketed the sky, with no sign of dawn's approach. She eased herself down beside him and covered them with their blankets. She rested her head beside his on the saddlebags and let her body relax as she fell asleep.

GEDRAN

Gedran struggled to sit up. The wounds on his back burned, the congealed blood and scabs stretching as he moved. He lacked the energy to attempt a healing spell. The lava pit beside him smelled of brimstone and sulphur. As he watched, leaning against the large rock, lazy bubbles of lava floated into the air and popped, sending droplets of lava flying at him. Trahern's creatures looked him over, checking the wounds, before judging him to be ready for travel. They bound his wrists in thick ropes, ensuring that he had no mobility in his hands. The small, goblin-like creatures weren't the same as the night before; the charred pig-snouted one who had taunted him appeared to have gone elsewhere. It took three of them to lift him. They hefted him up and threw him onto a hard saddle made of pale leather etched strange inked markings. The large, mangy black horse reeked of bile and blood.

The creatures tied the ropes around his wrists to the pommel of the saddle, forcing him into a sitting position.

The pain from his back radiated through him and he retched, emptying his stomach of what little bile remained there. He slumped to the side, leaning against the horse's neck in exhaustion. The strange caravan carried him closer to Trahern's stronghold in the center of the Shadowlands.

CHAPTER FOURTEEN

Roarke woke with the sunrise, the dim red glow of the strange sun disorienting him for a moment. Slowly, he noticed the weight on his right shoulder. He turned his head to the side and looked at Eislyn's face. Asleep, she looked like a child, the epitome of youth and innocence. The worries of the day were smoothed from her face, and a small smile curved her lips. He smiled at the sight of her, sleeping on his shoulder. He savored the moment of peace as he looked at her. Memories of his dream drifted across his consciousness and he cringed.

"Eislyn," he whispered, leaning close to her ear. "We have to get up now."

She mumbled in her sleep and smacked her lips, rolling away from him to pillow her head on the saddlebags. Roarke sat up, the stitches across his abdomen pulling despite the careful movements. He groaned, then gently grasped Eislyn's shoulder and shook her awake.

"Eislyn, you have to get up. Something is wrong."

"What's wrong? Did your stitches come undone?"

"Something happened to Gedran last night. I know this sounds crazy, but I dreamed about him. Trahern and his minions flayed him with a whip while he dangled over a pool of lava."

"That sounds terrible. It was just a dream, Roarke. It can't have been anything more than a dream."

"I don't know how to explain... I can feel that something is very, very wrong with Gedran right now, and I know that the dream was real. We have to find him, Eislyn." Roarke dug through his pack and saddlebags, searching for his father's maps, then flattened them out on the packed dirt. He studied them closely while Eislyn looked on, confused. "Here," he said, pointing at a vague smudge of red between two jagged lines. "This is where he was in the dream."

"But where are we?" Eislyn looked at the map, trying to determine where they were.

"I think we are here," he said, pointing to a group of jagged lines. "I think we are two days behind him, maybe three." He packed up the maps again and began filling the saddlebags and packs with everything they used the previous night.

"So we're going, even though you are injured," Eislyn said, staring at him.

"Yes, we can't wait for me to heal. It could take weeks. We have to go now." He blanched slightly as he saw the bloody cloths Eislyn had used to clean the gashes in his abdomen. He tossed them into the fire.

"Ok, then we go. But you have to promise me that you won't do anything stupid that could open the wounds again."

"I promise," Roarke said. He walked out of the shallow cavern where they camped and tossed the saddlebags onto the horses. He started to pull himself up into the saddle, then groaned and slid back down as pain ripped through his stomach, bringing him to his knees.

Eislyn raced to him, putting his arm around her shoulders and helping to support his weight. She kept her mouth shut, but helped him maneuver into the saddle and then mounted her own horse. Roarke held tight to the pommel of his saddle, swaying slightly.

"How bad is the pain?" Eislyn asked, looking at him.

"Worse than I thought it would be," he said.

Eislyn dug in her pack and retrieved a packet of feverfew. She handed him a leaf, grinning to herself when he looked confused.

"It's feverfew," she said. "Put it in your mouth and chew on it, then leave it tucked into your cheek for a few minutes before you swallow. It will help the pain."

He put the feverfew in his mouth and chewed, following her directions. After a few minutes, the pain in his abdomen began to lessen. He slumped in his saddle, gripping the pommel with both hands. Eislyn pulled up beside him and patted his mare before grabbing hold of the reins and leading them away from the rocky shelter.

A mist formed around them, diffusing the sunlight and making it impossible to judge the time of day. They rode for two hours before Eislyn noticed a familiar sight in the distance.

"Roarke, isn't that where we camped last night?" She pointed toward the silhouette of a jagged rock formation in the distance.

He looked where she pointed and shook his head. *Women,* he thought. *Da always said that he'd never known a woman who could find her way out of an open crate.*

"Eislyn, those can't be the same rocks. We rode off to the west earlier." He tried his best not to sound patronizing.

"Are you thick? Look at them. Really look. They are definitely the same rocks where we camped last night, and we are riding right back to them. This mist is making it impossible for us to tell which direction we're going."

"No, we aren't. You're being foolish."

"I am not being foolish. You are being an idiot." Her face reddened in frustration, appearing almost burgundy in the strange red sunlight. "We are going to end up right back where we started thanks to this damn mist."

"If you don't want to listen, if you'd rather argue, then go home, Eislyn. I don't need or want you here." He watched as her eyes flashed with anger.

"You don't... You are an idiot. I've saved your life twice, Roarke. Without me, you'd be those wyrmlings' dinner, assuming you made it past that rabid bear. I have done nothing but support and help you." She scowled, a deep crease forming between her delicate eyebrows.

"I don't need your help, Eislyn." The harsh tone of his voice was unlike the way he normally spoke to her. He knew he shouldn't speak to her that way, but he couldn't help it.

"Clearly, you do, or you'd have expired from blood loss last night."

"Why do you have to be so difficult?" Roarke growled deep in his throat. Frustration with her pigheadedness overwhelmed him.

"You must hate that I'm right. I'm not the one being difficult, Roarke. Those are the same rocks, and we have wasted two hours going in circles because of the mist. We have two options: ride there and discover I'm right, or turn around and go in the opposite direction, which gets us closer to your brother. You choose." She turned her horse and trotted off in the opposite direction.

"Eislyn, wait," Roarke said. He trotted after her. "I don't know what to say. I don't know how we got lost."

"We got lost because of this infernal mist that formed

after we set out. Everything I've read says that Trahern has defense mechanisms in place here that are meant to disorient travelers who dare to cross his borders."

"Why didn't you say that?"

"I did, but you weren't listening to me! You were too busy telling me I was wrong."

"I really thought you were."

"But I'm not, and I've fought beside you and saved your life. I deserve to be treated with respect, not underestimated because I'm female."

"You're right, and I'm sorry." Roarke looked chagrined, his eyebrows creased with worry that he had offended her.

"It's fine. But you need to remember that I came after you to help because I wanted to. I didn't want you to face this alone."

"I won't push you away again."

Eislyn reined in her horse for a moment, stopping to look at him. She reached out and placed her hand on his arm. Roarke smiled sheepishly at her, placing his hand over hers.

"Let's get going," he said, and they continued riding away from the rocks.

Their horses fell into a steady rhythm, and the clip-clopping of their hooves was the only sound in the preternaturally silent Shadowlands. The air felt thick and heavy with moisture, but no rain fell. Swirling dark clouds formed above them, white-hot bars of lightning dancing between them. Eislyn stopped abruptly to look up at the clouds, fascinated by the display the lightning was putting on.

"Have you ever seen a storm like this before?" She asked, transfixed by the beauty and ferocity of the clouds.

"No, I've never seen lightning without rain. It feels wrong."

"Everything about this place feels wrong. I can't put my finger on exactly why," Eislyn said, looking at Roarke.

"It's like Trahern has twisted everything here. Or the curse did." He reached across to pat her arm reassuringly. "We should get away from here before the lightning decides to strike the ground."

"You're probably right," she said, and spurred her horse forward.

They rode away from the storm. Behind them, a loud crack sounded, and the ground beneath them shook. Roarke looked over his shoulder to see a crack forming in the hard-packed ground as shards of dirt and rock exploded into the air, charred from the lightning's heat. He shivered despite the oppressive heat.

"That was way too close," he said. "I could feel the hairs rise up on the back of my neck when it hit the ground."

"Thank you for getting us out of there. I would have watched the lightning for hours. I was mesmerized."

"Everything in this place is designed to kill us."

"Everything I read, all those books... None of it compares to the reality of the Shadowlands. I know I gave that big speech earlier. But, Roarke..." She trailed off for a moment, her features sallow. "Roarke, I'm scared. I want to save Gedran and make it back home."

Roarke stopped beside her and grabbed the reins of her horse, pulling her to a stop and dragging them closer. He wrapped his arms around her, hugging her tightly.

"I know. I do, too. We will make it out of this alive," he said, stroking her back. He held her for a few moments, providing her as much comfort as he could, before releasing her and straightening in his saddle. "We need to get moving again."

Eislyn nodded and they began to ride again.

CHAPTER FIFTEEN

GEDRAN

Gedran woke, his body dangling from the saddle with his head resting against the matted black mane of the horse. He jumped, and the creature walking beside the horse hit him behind the knees with a long, straight stick.

Damn my pride, and everything else. I should have listened to Roarke, he thought to himself. *I'll never see him again, and I didn't tell him I love him. I'll never be able to tell him now.*

The horse plodded along slowly and Gedran let his mind wander, trying to remember little things about his parents, like his mother's smile and his father's laugh. He remembered how excited they were when he began showing promise in the magical arts.

Ma smiled at me, her eyes filled with pride when I lit the wood-stove from across the room. I'll never forget the way she ran to me and scooped me into her arms, spinning me around. I must have been five or six at the time. The Duke's portal master had come through town and lit candles in the schoolroom that way, the first of our lessons in magic and lore. He snuffed the candles out with another spell, then lit them again, saying the incantation so that we could learn it. I went home, and all of our candles were already lit, so I decided to try something a little bit bigger. Ma was so excited when I was successful. She and Da saved the money from the next two seasons' worth of wool to pay the portal master to give me extra lessons whenever he came to town.

A sharp jerk on the reins nearly unseated him, sending him back to the present.

"No sleep," the creature beside him grunted. "You stay awake now."

Gedran nodded to him, staring ahead blankly and becoming lost in thought again.

Didn't the portal master teach me something about family members being connected through magic? I think... Yes, he did. He told me a story about brothers who had been separated in the forest while out hunting. The younger brother, stronger in magic, was desperate and afraid, and he reached out to his brother with his mind. He showed him where he was hiding and told him of his fear as he cowered in a grotto formed by the gnarled roots of a large tree. His older brother searched for him, following the descriptions his brother had given him, and found him. They were much closer together than Roarke and I are, though. Roarke is in the cottage in Auguistin, and I'm... wherever this is.

It's got to be worth a try, he thought, deciding to try when they stopped for the evening. Despite being protected by Trahern, the creatures didn't travel once darkness began to fall. The misty sky made it difficult to tell where the sun was on the horizon, but Gedran suspected they were quickly running out of daylight. He sat in complete silence as they rode, determined to not give them any opportunities to hit him again when he couldn't defend himself. He bided his time until he heard the creatures begin to chatter. The horse stopped abruptly and Gedran slid backward from the saddle until the ropes binding him to the pommel caught him. The bones in his wrists ground together, and pain shot down his forearms as the ropes tightened. He dangled there for a few minutes before the creatures came to him, cutting the ropes free and leading him to a stake set in the rutted ground. They secured him to the stake, and he looked around, using the last moments of sunlight to get his bearings.

He slumped against the stake, picturing Roarke's face in his mind. He pictured each line and plane of his brother's face, even the scar just below his left ear from the day they tried to fight with real swords.

Roarke, he thought, pushing his mind toward the image of his brother in his head. *Roarke. You were right, this is no way to become a hero. I made it two days before Trahern's minions found me. He visited me that first night, after his creatures dangled me over a lava pool, and he flayed me with a whip that drained me of magic. I'm tied to a stake now, sitting beside a rock formation that looks like a wyrmling claw. I know that I'm going to die here, Roarke. I'm sorry for not listening to you. I valued my pride too much to lose and now it's going to cost me everything. I love you, little brother. I'm sorry. I wish there was a way to save me...*

He released the image of his brother from his mind, exhausted from the effort of projecting his mind toward Roarke. He dragged the ropes to the base of the stake and lay down on his side, pillowing his head on his arm. He fell asleep quickly, losing himself in a dreamless oblivion.

CHAPTER SIXTEEN

The shock of his brother's sudden presence nearly knocked Roarke out of the saddle. He startled fully awake at the sound of Gedran's voice in his head. He reined in sharply, nearly colliding with Eislyn as he focused on the sound of Gedran's voice describing the strange rock formation, shaped like a wyrmling claw. Roarke slumped in the saddle, burying his face in his mare's neck. A sob shook his shoulders, and Eislyn moved in close to him, rubbing his back gently. As Gedran's voice faded, emotion overcame him. He cried, all of the anxiety and fear that he locked inside his heart every day since the testing poured out from him in a torrent of tears. Gedran's last words, *save me*, echoed in his mind.

Eislyn rubbed his back and shushed him quietly, offering him the same comfort he had given her. As his tears began to slow, she stopped rubbing his back and waited for him to be ready to move on.

"Gedran," Roarke said quietly. "I heard his voice in my head, Eislyn, as clearly as I would have if he was right next to me. My dream about him... it was real. He talked about being flayed and told me that he's camped next to rocks shaped like a wyrmling's claw."

"Is there anything like that on your maps?" Eislyn asked him.

He shuffled through his saddlebags, digging out the maps. He held out the map of the Shadowlands to Eislyn, and she opened it.

"There," she said, "It looks like the wyrmling claw rocks are about a day's ride from where we started out. We aren't very far away from him, Roarke."

"What do we do?" He wiped the last vestiges of his tears from his face as he looked at her. Embarrassment filled him, but he could tell that she didn't judge him for it.

"Don't be thick, Roarke. We save him. Let's go." She folded the map again and handed it back to him so that he could stash it back in his saddlebags.

They started riding in the direction of the wyrmling claw rocks, further north than they had been initially heading. Roarke took a few breaths as they started out to calm his racing heart. The shock of being contacted by his brother had begun to wear off, but the anxiety remained. He knew that he'd need to be ready to fight when they found Gedran. He steadied himself, focusing on the horizon in the distance as they galloped until the horses were winded. They slowed to a walk and Roarke watched the landscape, scanning the area for the rocks they needed to find. The surrounding area became more rocky, and the mist seemed to fade around them.

"Where did the mist go?" Eislyn looked around, confused, as the sun became more clearly defined in the distance. It sat low on the horizon, twilight threatening its impending arrival with ominous maroon hues darkening the sky.

"I'm not sure, but we must be getting close to where they

are. I don't think Trahern would use the same type of tricks on his minions."

A loud scraping noise echoed around them. Roarke looked around for the source. Some of the rocks shifted closer to them, the scraping noise accompanying them. As they got closer, the cracks in the rocks became arms, and feral smiles formed in the rock faces.

"Ride," Roarke shouted to Eislyn as the first of the creatures approached them. "Ride!" He spurred his mare into a gallop, watching over his shoulder as Eislyn dug her heels into her gelding's flanks.

The horses sensed their riders' fear and shot forward, sprinting through the hellscape that surrounded them. Loud crunching and scraping noises continued to follow them, and loud bangs and thuds surrounded them as large rocks catapulted past them, crushing the few trees and plants that could grow in the barren landscape. Eislyn leaned from her saddle as she rode, slowing to a canter and grabbing a tree branch that stuck out of a pile of rubble. She stuck it between her back and the edge of the saddle, the rough bark scraping against her tunic, and readied herself to gallop again. One of the hulking creatures caught up to her, grasping her ankle in its rough stone fingers and pulling at her. She struggled to maintain her seat, reaching behind her for the branch and swinging it blindly toward the rock creature's face.

Roarke roared, screaming at the top of his lungs, as he watched Eislyn struggle with the rock creature. As he turned to ride back toward her, a resounding crack echoed as Eislyn struck the creature hard in the side of the head with the branch. Its grip loosened enough that she could pull her ankle free and she dug her heels into her horse's flanks, shooting forward in a gallop. They sped toward a gap in the rocky growth ahead of them, sweat from the exertion coating their mounts. They quickly outpaced the rock creatures, who had stopped to help their injured cohort. In the distance, a few short miles away, the silhouette of a wyrmling claw appeared on the horizon, just below the setting sun.

"Eislyn, look," Roarke said, pointing toward the silhouette in the distance.

"Almost there," she said. "Are you ready?"

"I don't think I can be more ready than I am right now. Either I save Gedran, or I die trying."

"Don't say that."

"It's true. I want you to promise me that you'll run if things start to go bad. Take my saddlebags and run."

"I'm not leaving you, Roarke."

"If it looks like I won't succeed, I need you to live. I won't be the reason you died, far from home on a failed quest to save my brother."

"I'm not leaving, you idiot. I love you."

Roarke looked stunned. He reined in his horse and stood still, staring at her.

"You love me." His voice sounded different, confused and a little happy.

"That's what I said."

"Then you definitely need to run if they take me down. Because I love you, too, and I want you to live. You deserve a better ending to your life than death in a desolate place, even if I die, too."

"I won't promise to leave, but I'll promise to consider it if it looks like you won't succeed. I need you to know, Roarke... I believe in you. I know that we are going to succeed in saving your brother. I know that we can do this." Her heart soared at his admission. She reached across the space between their horses and took his hand.

"I'm glad one of us is sure. Ready to go?"

"Time to save Gedran." Eislyn smiled at him, and they ran their horses toward the rocks.

CHAPTER SEVENTEEN

T he sound of hooves approaching the camp roused
Gedran. The Gorm surrounded him, searching the
horizon for the source of the noise.

"No one should be coming," the leader said. "Demon Lord
is not scheduled to visit tonight. He is having the stronghold
prepared for the ceremony. You two," he said, "scout the area
around the camp. Find the trespassers." It gestured to the
two creatures next to it, and they scattered, their snout-like
noses snuffling along the ground and in the air.

Gedran used a tiny amount of his magic to enhance his
hearing. He heard the whinny of horses and a woman's whisper, then the answering low rumble of a man's response. *That
sounded like... It couldn't be. Roarke isn't here,* he thought. He
listened closer, hearing his name, and his heart soared. *He is
here. My brother, after everything, came for me.*

After twenty minutes had passed, the leader of the creatures noticed that its two underlings hadn't returned. It
screeched, its snout quivering. As the hoofbeats got closer,
panic gripped the creatures and Gedran scooted back slightly,
putting himself just behind the post he was tethered to. The

sound of his brother's voice bolstered him, and he felt hope for the first time in days. He flexed his hands and wrists back and forth, stretching the leather ties to loosen them. *If I can just get free,* he thought, *I can try to find my daggers.*

"No, get weapons and stand still," The Gorm said, glaring at the others as they scurried about the camp. "No need to be scared. Demon Lord won't let us be hurt." He grabbed a club from the pile of weapons next to one of the rock claws and held it above his head; the others hurried to mirror him.

As the creatures grabbed their weapons, a pair of horses charged into the camp, the first rider swinging a massive sword. His first swing beheaded the closest of the creatures, sending it careening into the rocks. Gedran sat up straighter, flexing his wrists more quickly as he watched Roarke leap from the back of his horse. Roarke landed on his feet and swung his sword at the creatures that surrounded him, his muscular frame accentuated by the grace with which he moved. *He is practically one with the sword,* Gedran thought. *His skill is almost like magic. I've never seen anyone move that way.*

"Roarke," Gedran said, shock and pride coloring his voice. He watched as the other rider, a small woman in breeches, plucked a bow from the back of her saddle and nocked an arrow. She aimed and loosed, striking another of the creatures and sending it flying backwards with its momentum.

I wonder who she is, he thought. *Roarke never looked twice at any of the village girls. Where did he find her?* He watched, desperately trying to free himself from his bindings, as Roarke and the young woman battled against his captors. Roarke was a marvel with his sword, moving like a dancer among the creatures that surrounded him while the young woman took out those who were further away with her bow. He watched Roarke cut his way through the minions, wading through the fallen bodies to get closer to him. One of the creatures slashed Roarke's face with a dagger, and Roarke roared in rage and pain. He swung, slicing the creature nearly in two with his claymore. Another came at him with a shortsword, driving him to his knees with a brutal slash across his hamstring.

The leader of the creatures stood over Roarke, grinning maliciously.

"You came all this way to die, boy?" The creature mocked him, giggling menacingly. "Stupid boy. Better to let your brother sacrifice himself, yes? Better not to come here. But you came anyway. Tudras thinks that was a mistake."

Roarke spat at the creature. A maniacal grin spread across the creature's face and it hefted the club over its shoulder, the stony skin rippling as muscles bunched beneath it. As he prepared to swing, an arrow sprouted between his eyebrows. A shocked look spread across its face as his eyes filmed over and it fell backward. As their leader fell, the other creatures scattered in every direction, panic gripping them. The young woman picked off as many as she could as they scattered, only ceasing to shoot when the creatures had outrun the range of her arrows.

Roarke fell forward, the pain in his leg finally overwhelming him. Gedran screamed as his brother fell, panic overtaking him.

"No, Roarke, no. Stand back up," he said.

The young woman walked over to him and removed her belt knife. She sawed through the leather binding him to the stake.

He stood shakily, stumbling at first as his legs adjusted to moving again, then ran to his brother.

"Roarke," he said, rolling his brother onto his back. "Roarke. Look at me."

Roarke opened his eyes, and Gedran breathed a deep sigh of relief at seeing that his brother lived. He summoned as much of his magic as he could and funneled it into Roarke.

He gasped, arching his back as the magic wound its way through his body, healing the wounds on his face and thigh, as well as the partially-healed wounds from the wyrmling attack.

"Gedran," Roarke said, sighing as his body relaxed. "I found you."

CHAPTER EIGHTEEN

G edran carefully removed his hands from Roarke's arm, taking inventory of the wounds that began to knit back together before him. "You did. I'm not sure what possessed you to try, but I'm so glad you did. You saved my life."

Roarke struggled into a sitting position, and Gedran wrapped him in a hug. The young woman stood to the side, watching the two of them. She smiled at him as he glanced at her over Roarke's shoulder, then began to wander the camp, picking up her arrows and checking them over. He heard her humming quietly, a tune that tickled the edges of his memory.

"So, Roarke," Gedran said, curiosity about her finally overcoming his joy at seeing his brother, "who is she?"

"Do you remember the girl who held my hand at our parents' wake?"

"Yeah, sort of. Why?"

"That's her," Roarke said, smiling. "Eislyn. She's incredible, and funny, and smart, and..."

"And you love her," Gedran interjected. "I'd have to be blind not to see how you're looking at her right now."

"Yeah, I do. She tracked me for four days before she snuck into my camp while I slept and waited for me."

"She tracked you?" Though Gedran was careful to keep his face devoid of expression, shock filled his voice.

"She did. I'm not fully sure how she learned all these things, but she's well-read and seems to enjoy learning. A lot of the books she read about the Shadowlands helped us survive here. I wasn't happy when I woke up to find her in my camp, but I'm glad she found me. I don't think I'd have made it here if she hadn't." Roarke smiled at Eislyn, who stood awkwardly beside the horses as she put the salvageable arrows back into her quiver, trying not to stare at Roarke. He gestured her over, and she walked over to them, sitting on the ground beside him. He grabbed her hand and squeezed it.

"Gedran, this is Eislyn," he said.

"It's nice to meet you again, Eislyn. I'm lucky that - " Gedran's voice cut off as a portal opened behind him and a taloned hand pulled him backward.

Eislyn shrieked in terror.

"Foolish mortals," a deep voice said from within the swirling indigo portal. "You have no hope of success. By violating the treaty, your lives are forfeit, as is the sacrifice, and I will overrun your beloved Duchy with my minions." Maniacal laughter echoed through the night as the portal snapped closed, leaving a shimmering glow in the air.

Eislyn collapsed to the ground and Roarke ran to her, wrapping her in his arms. They sat for a while, resting among the carnage of the attack, before Eislyn stood. She helped Roarke to his feet, and the two of them began to clear the bodies out of the camp. They moved as many as they could from the central area to prepare a safe place for them to bed down for the night. Eislyn built a fire with more twigs from her pack as Roarke spread their bedrolls out, layering the blankets to make a thicker padding for Eislyn. After making sure all of the corpses were well clear of their camp, Roarke returned to the fire and sat down beside Eislyn. She leaned into him, resting her head on his shoulder as they stared at the fire.

Her stomach growled, and Roarke chuckled quietly. He reached over to his pack and grabbed a crusty piece of bread, some cheese, and some of the roasted venison they had cooked before they left Grainne. He set the bread to warm on the fire, then handed some of the cheese and meat to Eislyn. She leaned against him and stuck the salty smoked cheese into her mouth.

"Mmm," she said as she finished her bite. "I've always been a fan of smoked cheeses."

"Da loved to make them," Roarke said. "Gedran has his skill with it. He made this one a few weeks before the tournament and put it into our icebox." His face fell at the thought of his brother falling backward through the portal so soon after they caught up to him.

They continued their meal in silence, their closeness after the earlier revelations the only enjoyable part of the evening. The quest dragged on, and their failure cast a dark shadow across Roarke's hope to rescue Gedran from the Demon Lord.

CHAPTER NINETEEN

The dawn broke over the Shadowlands, casting an eerie red glow over the camp. Roarke rolled over as he woke, disoriented by the softness beneath his back. He sat up and looked around the camp, seeing the low-burning fire and Eislyn, propped against a large rock, leaning forward to rest her chin on her hand. She sat awake, staring into the distance. A small book sat in her lap; he could tell she spent part of her watch reading by the dim light of the fire while he slept.

"Good morning," she said quietly. "I hope you slept well."

"I wish I could say I had," Roarke said. "I just..."

"I know," she said, a small crease forming between her eyebrows as she frowned. "I can't stop picturing the relief on his face when he saw you, then the terror... The snap of the portal behind him... It made my blood run cold."

"I should never have let you come with me." Roarke stared at her. "I can't do this. We can't do this. The danger... it will only get worse from here. I won't risk you when I know we won't succeed."

"It isn't up to you," she said sternly, brows furrowed. "This is my life, Roarke. Mine. Not yours, not my father's, not my mother's. I left without a word to my family to follow you, despite knowing that you wouldn't want me here. I wasn't going to let you fight alone then. What makes you think that I'll let you push me out just because the situation gets more dangerous?" She raised her voice, her body shaking in anger and frustration. "I will not allow you to dictate what I do. I won't."

"Eislyn, I..."

"No." Her voice hardened, determination written across her face. "I don't want to hear excuses. I'm not some fainting princess who can't handle herself. I don't need saving. But Gedran does."

Roarke opened his mouth to speak, but shut it at a gesture of her hand.

"I know you love me. I know you want to protect me. I understand that. Did it ever occur to you that I might want to protect you, too? That I might need to be with you so that I can ensure that you survive?"

"I guess I hadn't thought about it that way," Roarke said, a chagrined look on his face. "I've been so desperate to make sure that nothing happens to you that... I guess I didn't realize that you might be just as determined to protect me. You're not like the other girls from the village."

Eislyn blushed. "Not at all," she said. "I never was."

"I don't know why I never noticed it before."

"No one did." She sighed. "I guess I thought that you had started to understand me during our travels together."

"It doesn't change the fact that this is a lost cause. We lost him already, he's with Trahern now. It's over, Eislyn."

"Are we dead?" She asked. "No. Then it isn't over, and we still have a chance." She smiled. "So, what are we going to do about Gedran? How can we find him now?"

"The creatures ran off in that direction when we

attacked," Roarke said, pointing off to the right. "It makes sense that they would run toward familiar territory where they knew they could find safety. We'll go that way and see what we can find from there." He pulled out the map from his pack and unfolded it, studying it carefully.

"Then what?"

"We hunt down and attack Trahern. He's the only one who could have summoned that portal. He must be holed up in his fortress." Roarke frowned. "We have to find the fortress."

"And when we do? How would we attack him?" Eislyn asked. "Nothing I've read has spoken of any weaknesses he possesses. I'm not even sure he can be killed."

"He has Gedran. There must be some reason that he's taking a magic user every generation. He needs something from them. He has to."

"Ok, so you think he needs something from Gedran to remain invulnerable?" Eislyn looked pensieve.

"I think that the magic he absorbs from magic wielders provides him a sort of protection that he doesn't have otherwise. Preventing him from draining Gedran will weaken him. If we can do that, we have a chance."

"I think we can. If we do, no one else will have to go through what Gedran is going through. No other siblings will have to worry or try to save their brother. No one else will be sacrificed. But how will we find him?" Eislyn said, grabbing Roarke's map from him.

"It looks like Trahern's fortress is northeast of here," Roarke said, pointing to a rough sketch toward the right corner of the map. "Based on where we are now and the direction the creatures ran, I think they headed back toward Trahern."

"We should look through the things they left behind," Eislyn said. "Now that it's light out we can get a good idea of what kind of supplies we inherited during your hostile takeover of the camp."

The two of them ransacked through the sacks of supplies, tossing aside the strange blood-red foodstuffs they found. Roarke sniffed the contents of a waterskin to check if it was drinkable, then gagged. He poured it out, revealing an odd pink liquid with gelatinous chunks floating in it.

Eislyn's stomach heaved at the sight of the liquid spilling. "Please don't do that again," she said. "It would be better to not use their waterskins than to see what disgusting concoction was inside of them."

Roarke nodded, determined to ignore the bile at the back of his throat, and discarded the remaining waterskins without checking them. He sat heavily on the ground, picking through the contents of a larger sack, when he heard Eislyn yell.

"What?" Roarke shouted.

"I found a map," she said, laying it out on the ground and pinning down the corners with rocks so that they could take a closer look at it. A hot wind picked up from the south as the sun rode higher into the sky, rustling the fabric of the different sacks of supplies as Roarke laid out his map and sat down beside Eislyn to compare them.

"Here is where we are right now," Roarke said, pointing to a spot marked on the map with a red splotch; beneath the red splotch was a drawing of a claw. "This spot here, that's the lava fissure where Trahern was torturing Gedran in my dream. I think, based on how this map is drawn, that this," he pointed at a spot in the north-central part of the map, marked with a circle bisected with vertical lines, "is Trahern's stronghold. It makes sense, and it fits more closely with the direction the creatures ran off in last night." He leaned in closer to the map, tracing his fingers over the claw and circle, attempting to measure the distance.

"I think you're right," Eislyn said, watching him as he studied. "This spot here, the one that looks like a leaning letter T? It looks like the rock formation where we camped the first night after we were attacked by the wyrmlings."

"I think you're right," Roarke said. "The shape on the map is very similar to what I remember. Not that I remember too much after the attack… I still don't know how I survived."

"I guess you're just lucky that I followed you," Eislyn said. "I read several books on herbal healing and packed my medicinal herbs and bandages so that I could patch you up if anything happened." She smirked at him. "Looks like it was a good idea, after all."

"That's what you keep saying," Roarke teased. "It seems like I'm even luckier than I thought, since you love me."

"And you love me. Now we just have to make it out of here alive, with your brother in tow." She leaned against him, resting her head against his arm. "Based on the distance between where we camped last and here, it looks like we are about a day's ride from Trahern's stronghold now," Eislyn said.

"I think the smartest thing we can do is travel most of the way there today, then make camp for the night. That way we aren't arriving at his stronghold late in the day and weary from travel," Roarke said.

"Being road weary will not be an advantage for us when it comes to wielding magic or weapons against him. Are we decided, then?" Eislyn asked.

"Wielding magic?" Roarke looked incredulous.

"Well… yes," she said. "You're not the strongest in the duchy, but you are capable of basic spells. Aren't you?"

"I don't know anything remotely useful. I can barely summon a flame to start a fire."

"We don't know what will be useful. Nobody has seen

Trahern, other than the sacrifices, for centuries. What can you do?"

"I can summon a spout of water, make a small flash of light, and heal very minor wounds. Nothing useful," Roarke said, embarrassment coloring his cheeks crimson.

"I don't know, a small flash of light could be useful as a distraction," Eislyn said, "and Gedran will be able to help us, once we get to him."

"You hope."

"I hope. We will find him again, Roarke. We've done it once, and we will do it again." She sounded fierce and determined.

"I wish I was as confident as you are. We probably should get started."

They finished sorting through the supplies left behind by the creatures who had fled during the attack, gathering everything that was usable and dividing it between their saddlebags. Luckily, the horse that Gedran had ridden had been left behind by the creatures, tied to a protruding rock on the side of the formation. Roark tossed an extra set of saddlebags across the back of the horse and tied the reins to his pommel, then walked the horses over to where Eislyn sat atop her gelding. Packed and ready, they rode away from the campsite, not bothering to hide the evidence of their presence this time.

CHAPTER TWENTY

A scream echoed through the stone courtyard at the center of Trahern's fortress, interrupting the silence inside the antechamber that led to his rooms. The vision pool, once swimming with color as he studied it, went dark and he whipped his head around to locate the sound.

The Gorm leader approached him, attempting to make himself small and innocuous as he got closer. *What's his name again?* Trahern thought. *Putrus? Tumnus?*

"M-Master," the Gorm stuttered, "the prisoner is secured, as you requested."

"Good," Trahern said, his face devoid of expression.

"Tudras is honored to serve, Master."

Ah, Tudras, that's the name, Trahern thought.

"Master?" Tudras said, snapping Trahern out of his reverie. "Do you need something?"

"What should Tudras do now? The prisoner is in place."

"So you said," Trahern snapped. "Go to your hovel and lash yourself twelve times for boring me with your repetition."

"Yes, Master." The creature stumbled from the room, clumsy in its haste to escape.

Trahern chuckled to himself, pleased to see the Gorm's fear and obeisance. He turned back to the vision pool, breathing through a small pipe and staring at the tranquil water. The surface rippled twice before becoming as smooth as glass. An image appeared before him.

The interlopers searched the camp where the Gorm held the sacrifice, digging through saddlebags and satchels left behind when the cowardly creatures bolted after the male stormed the camp. *The fools, leaving behind so many supplies,* Trahern thought, watching as the companions located a map within one of the bags. He threw the pipe down, unleashing an otherworldly howl of rage. The pool went black, its surface like polished onyx, all traces of the vision wiped away.

Trahern stormed into his chambers, grabbing his whip from its hook by the door. He cracked it overhead and bared his teeth in an unnatural imitation of a smile.

"Someone is going to pay for this," he growled, stalking toward the courtyard where his sacrifice hung from a slab of rock. "Starting with you."

CHAPTER TWENTY-ONE

Tudras hid behind a large clay pot just outside Trahern's antechamber, holding its breath. It winced as it heard a whip crack from within, shrinking back further into the shadows. It felt the door slam, shaking the stone walls from the impact.

Master is angry, he thought. *Tudras must be very careful not to anger him more.* It watched as Trahern's whip dragged by on the cobblestone floor toward the courtyard. Trahern shouted, his voice muffled by the walls and the clay pot.

Nononononononono... Must hide. Must not let Master see me here. The whip cracked again, and a pained scream reverberated through the stone halls. Tudras scrambled away, its head down as the sound of the whip chased it from the corridor. It held its breath while it rounded the corner, moving as quickly as its clumsy feet would allow. The door leading to the hall where the Gorm kept their quarters loomed in front of it, slightly ajar, and it ran through.

The coppery scent of wyrmling blood and woodsmoke filled the air. *Home,* it thought. It slowed from its frenetic pace, nodding in acknowledgment at the other Gorm as it passed.

Pulling aside the tattered fabric that surrounded its sleeping area, Tudras slipped inside and knelt beside the pallet on the ground, feeling beneath it for the leather handle of the short, metal-tipped whip. Removing its roughspun shirt and folding it carefully, it gripped the thick handle and swung backward over its shoulder. The cold metal of the thong cracked into the stony skin of its back, an angry welt forming where it struck.

"One," Tudras said, its breath hissing out through gritted teeth as it raised the whip again. The metal sank into its skin, putrid black blood seeping from the wound. "Two."

CHAPTER TWENTY-TWO

The sulfuric smell of molten rock wafted from the fissures in the ground. Roarke carefully steered his mare around the cracks in the rutted ground to avoid the bubbles of lava that escaped. Eislyn followed closely behind him on her mount, leading the spare horse, determined to stay close. The further north they went, the darker the sky became. The blood-red sun absorbed the ambient light surrounding it, no longer giving off light itself. Billowing black clouds floated across the sky. A chill came over Roarke, raising gooseflesh on his skin despite the heat.

Maybe we shouldn't be doing this, he thought to himself. *The further we go, the more disturbing the landscape becomes.* Trunks of dead trees twisted together like the braids of the little girls in their village; a rock formation that resembled a mouth, screaming in twisted agony stood beside the interwoven trees, black viscous liquid oozing from cracks in the rock.

An otherworldly shrieking noise filled the sky, piercing their ear drums as they rode. It increased in pitch and Eislyn shook as panic gripped her. Slumping down into her saddle, she curled into herself and covered her ears with her hands, a sharp keening noise ripping from her throat. Roarke rushed to her and quickly grabbed her horse's reins.

"Shush, Eislyn, it's ok," he said, holding her horse still. "Shh, it's ok." He reached across the space between their horses and lightly stroked her upper back between her shoulder blades, trying to soothe her.

The distress on her face felt like an arrow through his heart. Still holding her reins, he dismounted and pulled her into his arms, She leaned into Roarke, taking the offered comfort, and nuzzled close to him. They stayed there, still and quiet, for several minutes, until Eislyn pulled away and remounted her horse.

"We should keep going," she said. "I'm sorry for letting the noise get to me. I know we have to hurry."

"It's fine, Eislyn. The shrieking was getting to me, too," Roarke said, his brow furrowed in concern. "I will probably hear it in my dreams if we make it out of here alive."

He hopped back into his saddle and the two of them started off again, carefully picking their way around the lava-filled crevices in the rocky ground. The strange darkness continued to grow around them, and the popping and bubbling sounds of the lava grew louder as they approached a narrow rock bridge over a wide chasm. Roarke rode toward the side to get a better view of the bridge, but his mare shied away, refusing to go closer. He dismounted and strode to the edge. The thin rocky ledge appeared brittle. Roarke chucked a rock at it; the rock hit and skidded, sending a shower of tiny rock shards down into the lava.

"I'm going to go first. Please don't cross until I'm on the other side," Roarke said, turning around to face Eislyn. "I don't think it can hold the weight of more than one of us at a time."

"We'll have to leave Gedran's horse here," Eislyn said. "I

won't be able to ride across and bring him with us if it won't withstand the weight."

Roarke nodded. "There's no safe way to get him across."

Eislyn dismounted from her gelding, keeping hold of the other mount's reins and leading him to a nearby tree. She tied him to a sturdy branch and stroked his muzzle, shushing him softly. "Okay," she said. "Let's go."

Roarke nodded and turned back around. He carefully walked his horse across the narrow stone bridge, ears on alert for any sign of trouble. As he stepped off the bridge and pulled up to the side of the chasm, Eislyn began to cross, her horse stepping carefully on the brittle rock. Shards of rock fell from the bridge into the lava, and a strange growling noise echoed beneath the bridge. Eislyn rode faster, rushing across the bridge as the noise increased and the stone began to shake. As she landed on the other side, a large rumble echoed, followed by the sound of splintering as the rock bridge shattered and fell into the lava. The ground quaked beneath them, and the fissures surrounding the chasm widened, the lava bubbling to the surface. Roarke and Eislyn spurred their horses to a gallop in their desperation to get away from the earthquake.

"No going back now," Eislyn said.

"I guess not," Roarke said. "Together?"

"Together," Eislyn said.

As they rode further away, the aftershocks of the earthquake lessened. In the distance, a loud crashing noise sounded, followed by the agonized scream of a creature trapped by falling rock. The discombobulating mist shrouded the sun and further diffused the light. A veil of shadows fell over the landscape.

"The mist is back," Eislyn said.

"Not again," said Roarke, looking up at the darkened sky. "We need to do something to keep from getting lost again."

Eislyn dismounted and marked the ground with a stick, scratching her initials into the ground with its broken end. When she finished, she wiped her hands on her breeches and looked up at Roarke.

"How's that?"

"Perfect. Hopefully nothing will hide it." Roarke slid from his saddle and dug into the ground with his fingers, deepening the grooves of Eislyn's initials and filling one of them with small rock shards. "That should help."

They climbed back into their saddles and moved on, riding past piles of bones and the gore of bodies ripped limb from limb. The landscape began to change as they got closer to Trahern's stronghold, becoming more lush and vibrant. Humidity thickened the air, combining with the mist to create an oppressive tropical heat. Sweat dripped down Roarke's back, leaving an uncomfortable trail of moisture on the thin linen of his shirt. Strange plants grew around the fissures in the rocky ground and wrapped themselves around the decrepit trunks of long-dead trees. The stink of rot and bile filled the air, emanating from the overblown flowers that bloomed from the vines and stalks surrounding them. Roarke hopped down and crouched, marking the ground by dragging the tip of his dagger across the rocky surface. Eislyn looked around, studying the strange plants that bloomed in the otherworldly oasis that marked the far edge of Trahern's stronghold. As she watched, one of the flowers snapped open, revealing rows of sharp, feral teeth. She jumped, unsettling her horse and nearly unseating herself. Roarke grabbed hold of her horse and gave her time to steady herself again.

"You okay?" Roarke looked up at her, studying her face.

"That flower.... The bright pink one. It has teeth, Roarke. Teeth." She shivered as she pointed out the flower she had noticed.

Roarke looked up at the flower, watching as it snapped

open again, revealing row after row of teeth. It snapped shut with a clattering noise. He yipped in surprise.

"What other strange things are we going to see here?" He shuddered. "A flower with teeth. Did you ever read anything like that, Eislyn?"

"No, I haven't. I didn't think something like that could be possible." She looked down at him and he patted her leg. She watched him climb back into his saddle, and they moved on together, carefully skirting around the plants that stretched toward them from their stems.

They picked their way through the overgrown land, keeping their eyes focused on the hazardous landscape surrounding them. The lava fissures hid beneath the large leaves and wove between tall stalks of flowers that gave off the stench of rotting meat. Eislyn gagged at the scent and Roarke held his breath as they passed beneath large flowers that hung low from the tall stalks growing around them. One flower stretched toward Eislyn, snapping its petals like jaws as she spurred her gelding to a canter, narrowly avoiding its maw. In the distance, the outline of a large building appeared on the horizon, dark against the crimson sky.

"I think that's it," Eislyn said, pointing toward the building.

"I think you're right," said Roarke. "Let's go a little further and find a spot to camp for the night."

They wove through the tall stalks and rotting detritus that lined the rocky ground, moving deeper into the dismal oasis that thrived around them. Roarke reviewed their surroundings for something, anything, that could provide them with a safe shelter for the night. A group of dead stalks stood a short distance away, leaning against one another near a large, barren tree with knots covering its trunk.

That could work, Roarke thought. *We could lean the stalks against the tree, if there are enough of them, which would give us an actual shelter. There should be enough twigs and leaves to build a fire, too.* He studied it more closely as they approached.

"I think this is it," he said, pointing to the leaning stalks.

"That's a great idea," Eislyn said. "We can use the stalks and the tree to form a lean-to."

Roarke rode toward the stalks to get a closer look. The stalks swayed, despite the lack of a breeze, making an eerie clacking noise that masked all other sound. A small, furry creature darted out from beneath the stalks, leaping at Roarke. Its fangs latched into his thigh, and he snatched his belt knife from its sheath at his waist, stabbing the overgrown rodent in the neck. The shock of the blade made it release its jaw, and he flung it aside.

"I think that was a Ratatoskar," Eislyn said. "I've read about them in a few books about the Shadowlands. They aren't supposed to be poisonous, but we should definitely clean the wounds quickly." She dug through her saddlebags, searching for the medicinal herbs and her sewing pouch. "I'll need... hmm... It figures we'd encounter something I don't know exactly how to treat and he'd be bitten, so now I have to figure it out," she grumbled to herself absentmindedly as she searched through the pouches of herbs in her kit.

"Do you have to talk about me like I'm not here?" Roarke asked. "I'm right here, and you're complaining about me being bitten by something I didn't even know was there."

"I'm sorry, but I have to figure out how to fix you, yet again, despite having no idea whether the information I've read about that creature is accurate. I suppose you have some input, since you're so knowledgeable about herbs?" Eislyn countered.

"Feverfew? I would love a couple leaves to dull the pain. Those fangs hurt," Roarke said, his voice serious.

Eislyn smiled at him, then dug the packet of feverfew out of her pack and handed him a few leaves. He stuffed them in his mouth and chewed, then stuck them into the hollow of his cheek to sit. Eislyn cleared the area, ensuring that no other rodents were hiding in the area they planned to camp. She drew her bow and kept an arrow nocked, prepared to shoot if any hostile creatures appeared. A loud rustling noise came from their left, and she loosed her arrow. It struck the trunk of a nearby tree after passing through the clattering stalks. As the arrow hit, she noticed the light breeze blowing through the area, creating the susurration that startled her. She looked around frantically to see if Roarke had noticed the errant arrow. Embarrassment colored her cheeks as she returned to where he rested, but she was pleased to have cleared the campsite without any other rodents or creatures found. She sat beside Roarke, who rested with his back against the twisted trunk of the tree, their horses tethered a short distance away.

"All clear," she said. "I've got my herbs and equipment ready; why don't you slide over here and we can get started cleaning your leg up?"

Roarke rode over and climbed carefully from the saddle, avoiding hitting his injured leg. Eislyn pulled the dead stalks from the ground, setting them in a criss-crossing pattern to create a lean-to above where Roarke rested, then arranged a set of small rocks into a circle and built a fire. She filled their small metal pot with water from one of the waterskins and placed it on the logs. She carefully measured out herbs and dropped them into the pot with the water, bringing it to a boil. Roarke watched as she prepared everything, then dipped the clean pieces of linen into the herbal concoction. She blew on the linen to cool it slightly. Roarke pulled his breeches down to expose the wound, thankful for the breechcloth that kept the rest of him covered. The steam from the pot smelled of feverfew and eucalyptus, raising a scent memory from his early childhood: soft hands and a warm cloth gently cleaning a large scrape on his knee. *Mother,* he thought. He hissed as the boiled water on the cloth touched the deep gouges, jolting him from his reverie and taking his breath away. He grasped the bedroll tightly in one hand, closing his eyes tightly to avoid seeing the damage.

Eislyn cleaned his wounds, humming quietly while she worked. The gentle tones of her song soothed him, despite the pain pulsing in his thigh. "I'm going to have to stitch the big one closed," she said. "I'm so sorry. You've gotten so many new scars since I found you." She held her needle over the flames to sterilize it.

"It's ok. I don't mind scars," Roarke said, his teeth gritted as the hot metal slid into his skin..

"Me neither, but I don't like when you hurt," Eislyn said, laughing quietly. "Do you have any pain, Roarke?"

"Not anymore."

"That's the most important thing," Eislyn said.

Roarke leaned closer to the fire, holding his hands out to warm them. While Eislyn stitched up his leg, the sun descended into twilight, bringing a chill over the camp. As she tied off the final suture and clipped the string, he stretched, then stood to slide his breeches back into place. Slipping his arm around her shoulders as he sat back down, he scooted her closer to him. She put the needle and scissors back into the pouch and leaned her head against him, holding her hands out and flexing her fingers in the warmth from the dancing flames. They sat in silence for some time, warming themselves and resting. The battle with Trahern loomed on the horizon.

CHAPTER TWENTY-THREE

Trahern sat beside the vision pool, trailing his fingers through the water. The sacrifice's screams had silenced some time before as he fell unconscious. *A pity,* Trahern thought, *I was just beginning to enjoy myself.* The siphoned magic surged through his veins, strengthening him. A humming euphoric sensation filled him.

The surface of the pool rippled, colors dancing across it, forming shapes and moving through scenes of the two interlopers. Trahern watched as they entered the rotting oasis at the outer edge of his fortress grounds.

"They approach, despite the perils. Fools. The treaty is void," he growled. "Once the sacrifice is drained, I will drain the pitiful male who followed him, then march upon Amadan with the full might of the Shadowlands behind me."

He strode to the door and stared into the courtyard. The sacrifice hung limply from his wrists, scraps of his shirt dangling from his thin frame. The Demon Lord heaved a sigh and turned back to the pool. The man's face, so similar to the sacrifice's, shimmered on the surface.

"Yes," he said, staring at the reflection. "Come to my fortress, foolish mortals. Come and meet your end."

CHAPTER TWENTY-FOUR

Roarke watched as the sun peeked over the horizon. He thought back to the previous night, remembering Eislyn's anxiety and desire to take the first watch. He knew she feared what lay before them; he did, too. As he watched the dawning of the new day before him, he thought to himself, *I wonder if this will be the last sunrise I'll see. By tomorrow morning, we might all be dead.*

He shook off the depressing thought and focused on stoking the fire to prepare their breakfast. *I wonder if any of Eislyn's herbs would be good for tea,* he thought. *Why haven't I asked her that before?* He pulled the last of the bread and cheese from his pack, breaking it into three pieces and placing the bread on the stones beside the fire to warm. He grabbed strips of the roasted venison, which now had the texture of jerky, and warmed those, as well. He sat beside Eislyn and pulled his journal out of his pack as he waited for the food to heat. Glancing at her face, he felt an involuntary tug on his heartstrings. He grabbed his pen and began to write.

Only two nights have passed since we tried to save Gedran from Trahern's minions. Before Trahern pulled him back through the portal, he seemed... different. He struggled to heal me, despite his years of practice. My magical abilities are more limited, but I can feel the drain on my stores as we sit here. To know how he must feel, having his very essence stripped away... the pain must be nearly unbearable. Yet he still tried to survive here, and we almost succeeded at saving him.

Eislyn is trying to remember the exact prophecy that Trahern was given. Books from that time are scarce, even in a noble's library, which makes it difficult to know if she's seen the true words of the prophecy before or not. We will fight him, regardless of what the prophecy says, but it would be nice to know if he has a weakness that can be exploited. She recalls reading that his downfall will be due to the strongest man in the human lands. She believes this to be why Trahern's treaty with Duke Grainne requires the strongest magic wielder from each generation be sacrificed. Historically, the strongest men in human history have been extraordinarily strong with magic, far exceeding their peers in each generation.

If strength in magic is what will defeat Trahern, that may explain why everything within the Shadowlands seems to drain at our stores of magic. From what Gedran told us, he wasn't found by Trahern's minions until four days after he came through the portal. Having a spell woven to drain magic stores from humans within the realm would allow Trahern to ensure that his sacrifice was sufficiently weakened before arriving at his fortress. If the sacrifice is drained, he will be unable to attack Trahern with any success. The only other option, which is what I'm hoping for, is that the prophecy has been interpreted incorrectly for centuries. If that is the case, then we have a chance.

Roarke heard a cough and looked up. Eislyn sat up and smiled at him. Roarke smiled back, tossing a piece of warm bread to her.

"Good morning," Eislyn said. "You already warmed up breakfast?"

"I figured it would be helpful if it was ready when you woke up."

She rolled her eyes at Roarke. "You're trying to make up for all the times you woke me up."

"I'm sorry for waking you up too early every day," Roarke said. He held out another chunk of warm bread and one of the pieces of cheese as a peace offering. During their time traveling together, he learned to tread carefully in the mornings; Eislyn didn't wake up easily.

She sat up and took the bread and cheese, taking a large bite from the bread and sighing. She chewed quietly, staring into the low flames of the fire.

"You were writing," she said.

"I was," Roarke responded.

"I read it, you know. Your journal."

"You what?" Roarke hastily put the small book back into his pack, tossing a glare at Eislyn. "Why would you do that?"

"I had been following you for days, and I wanted to know why you were running. When I got to your camp the night before you found me, you were asleep with the journal on the ground beside you. I read through part of it to find out what was going on."

"But it's my thoughts. My private thoughts."

"I'm sorry, Roarke. I shouldn't have read it, but if I hadn't, I wouldn't have known what I was getting into. Please don't be angry with me."

"I didn't think anyone would ever read it, unless..."

"Unless you didn't make it," Eislyn said, a sober look on her face.

"Yes."

"Well, we are going to make it, and I did read it. In the end, that doesn't matter at all. We need to defeat Trahern. To do that, we need a plan."

"Ok, then let's plan. How do we want to do this?" Roarke asked.

"Based on the map and where we stopped yesterday, it looks like we are about an hour and a half's ride away from the bridge that crosses over the stronghold's moat," Eislyn said. "Based on everything I've read, the area closest to the bridge will be more heavily fortified with Trahern's creations. We can expect resistance before we get to Trahern."

"Are you sure you're from Auguistin? How could you have read so many books?" Roarke teased.

"I'm sure," Eislyn said, laughing. "My mother values reading, and my father buys whatever books he can find for her. I've read everything in their library, as well as the books that my brothers brought home from school."

"There are books on the Shadowlands at the village school?" Roarke sounded incredulous.

"Oh, no, those we found on the peddler's wagon, or when Father would travel to purchase goods he needed for the shop."

"That makes a lot more sense," Roarke said. "I can't picture the schoolmaster allowing anyone to read something that would taint their view of the treaty."

"You're right. The Duke wouldn't allow it. How are we going to do this, Roarke?" Eislyn asked as she packed her bedroll and blanket.

"Ok, so we need to consider that the one and a half hour time frame might be longer, depending on how many of Trahern's creatures we run into. We shouldn't dally here for too long." Roarke said, then stood and began to gather up the small odds and ends and put them away in packs and saddlebags.

Roarke offered a hand to Eislyn, helping her up from where she sat beside the last embers. She buried the fire as he rolled the bedrolls and placed them behind their saddles. As they packed up the camp, his gaze drifted back to Eislyn, watching as she brushed her hair away from her face. Her wit and intelligence captivated him. Her stubbornness drove him mad.

I wouldn't be here without her, he thought to himself. He smiled at her, and she caught his eye, returning his smile. *We have to defeat Trahern. After that... I guess we'll have to figure out exactly what comes next.* He looked around the camp. Eislyn had loaded the last of the saddlebags onto the horses. Roarke walked to her and gathered her close for a hug.

"Are you ready?" Roarke asked.

"As ready as I can be. Let's get going," Eislyn said, stroking her gelding's mane.

The duo climbed into their saddles, heading along the path of fissured cracks toward Trahern's stronghold. The smell of sulfur and the stench of rotted meat followed them as they wove their way through the otherworldly forest. Roarke stretched his arms above his head, rolling his shoulders back to work out the ache that formed at the base of his neck. The scenery of the forest changed slightly around them, the deciduous trees getting taller with full leaves that rustled in the hot breeze. Ahead of them, crackling and popping noises escaped the fissures as lava began to bubble and splash over the edges.

Eislyn shrieked as a lava bubble struck her in the leg, just above her boot. The scalding molten rock burned through her breeches and left a raised blister on her thigh. She pressed her hand against the wound and moaned low in her throat, trying to stifle the pain. The sound of her scream echoed through the forest. As the echo faded, a new rustling began, followed by chittering and the sound of gnashing teeth.

"What is that?" Roarke shouted.

Eislyn panted as she dug through her pouch for a feverfew

leaf. "I don't know, but it doesn't sound good. Something is coming."

As she spoke, a score of large creatures skittered into view. Eight-legged, with wide, hourglass-shaped bodies and large, clicking mandibles, the strange creatures ran toward Eislyn, following the direction of her scream.

"Arachnes. Those are Arachnes," Eislyn said as she grasped her leg, holding the chewed feverfew against the blister.

Roarke leapt from his horse, drawing his sword and plunged into the fray, brutally hacking his way through the Arachnes. Blood and ichor sprayed from the wounds, and Roarke freed his belt knife and slashed at another one as he ripped his sword free. Grabbing it, he spun, blades flashing and slicing into the Arachnes that surrounded him. One of the creatures leapt at him, digging its mandible into his arm. He screamed, pulling it from his arm and flinging it away from him. It hit the tree with a sickly crunch and fell to the ground, still.

Eislyn watched as Roarke swung his sword, cutting an Arachnes in two and sending the pieces flying toward more of the creatures. Bodies piled up around him as he worked his way back toward her. She still sat astride her horse, her face pale from pain. He backed up to her, defending her from the creatures with his blade while she restrung her bow and nocked an arrow.

She loosed one arrow, then another, then another, cutting down the remaining Arachnes as they skittered toward them. As the final creature fell, Roarke turned to Eislyn, gently shifting her pants left to the side to inspect her wounded thigh. The angry red weal blistered with several pockets filled with liquid. She gasped as he probed the area around it with the tips of his fingers, trying to determine how far the blistering had gone. He squinted, focusing hard on his meager stores of magic and poured a trickle into the wound, easing the pain slightly and providing a cooling sensation that would enable her to ride again.

"That's all I can do for now," he said, patting her knee gently before walking to his horse to grab a piece of cloth from his saddlebags. He dabbed at the wound on his forehead, wiping the blood and dirt away from the gash. "I don't have Gedran's skill with healing or your skill with herbs."

"I know," she said, catching his hand and holding it tightly. "But you healed me just the same. Thank you."

"Sure," Roarke said. "You're welcome." As the adrenaline faded, he became aware of the piercing pain above his left ankle. Looking down, he saw the rip in his boot and the bloodstains on the leather. He sat down heavily, removing his boot and inspecting the damage to his leg. A long, shallow gash ran across his leg; the bleeding appeared minimal. He grabbed a roll of bandages and wrapped some around his leg, tying it off, and put his boot back on.

"Are you okay to continue now?" Roarke asked as he walked back toward his horse.

Eislyn nodded, focused on the Arachnes that attacked them. Roarke, satisfied that they could move on, climbed back into his saddle. They took off toward the stronghold. No other obstacles appeared to them as they approached the bridge to Trahern's stronghold, and Roarke, emboldened by his success at fending off so many of the Arachnes, readied himself for the fight. He charged across the bridge, reaching the steps of the stronghold, then jumped from the saddle.

"TRAHERN!"

CHAPTER TWENTY-FIVE

The ground quaked beneath them as the gates ground open with a loud, grating rumble. A strange glow the color of dying embers emanated from the crack forming between the gates. As the gap got wider, the silhouette of a large, hulking creature appeared. Eislyn gasped.

"Is that..." she asked, trailing off.

"That's him. It has to be."

Roarke growled low in his throat. He moved forward, Eislyn grabbed his arm to stop him.

"Wait," she said. "He's coming out. Let him come to us."

Roarke grunted. He stood silently, staring at the silhouette as it slowly came into focus. Trahern seemed to suck the glow around him into himself, appearing as a shadow wreathed in flame-colored light as he stood in the door of the fortress.

"Why isn't he saying anything?" Roarke wondered aloud.

Eislyn shook her head, equally confused. Roarke drew his sword, slamming it into the ground. The loud clang hung in the air. Trahern's laughter echoed around them.

"You think to challenge me, little boy?" Trahern asked, his gravelly voice hard. The breeze shifted, and he sniffed the air. "You smell of fear and anger, and," he paused, "hardly any magic to speak of. Come. Enter my fortress and see what has become of so many of your kind."

"We don't need magic to end you, demon," Roarke said, filling his voice with every ounce of disdain and anger he possessed. He swung his sword in a showy arc, staring down Trahern across the bridge. He strode forward purposefully.

"No, Roarke. Don't." Eislyn's face appeared calm, but the fear in her voice betrayed her.

Trahern laughed again. "No, Roarke," he said, imitating Eislyn's voice. "Listen to your delectable little mate. She is much, much smarter than you." As he raised his arms, the horns that curled from his forehead became wreathed in flame, illuminating the gaunt planes of his face. Eislyn squeaked, stepping her horse backward a few steps at the sight of Trahern's skeletal visage.

"Eislyn, draw your bow and be ready," Roarke said, staring at Trahern.

She drew her bow and nocked an arrow, her hands shaking slightly. Roarke stood, straight-spined and strong, mere feet from the entrance to the fortress. The red sunlight glinted off of the claymore in his hands. Trahern turned, walking casually back through the stronghold's gates, flicking his whip back and forth.

A noise behind them set Eislyn on high alert. She whipped around, loosing an arrow and striking the pig-snouted creature in the chest. As it fell backward, several others began to appear from the woods. Their snouts quivered as they sniffed the air, scenting the blood of their fallen cohort. A collective wail of rage sounded in the air, and the creatures charged.

"Roarke," Eislyn screamed. "Go!"

Roarke turned, seeing the creatures charging toward them, and ran into the fortress with Eislyn close on his heels. Trahern stood in the center of the stone courtyard, his glowing whip unfurled. A taunting smile stretched his face, contorting it into a villainous mask. Behind him, Gedran dangled by his wrists, lash marks visible across his body. Roarke swung his sword in a tight arc, then tossed it from one hand to another as he regarded the infamous Demon Lord. A wry smile crossed his lips.

"Are you coming or not?" Roarke asked Trahern.

Trahern laughed, a deep rumble that reminded Roarke of the earthquake they had witnessed as they crossed the brittle stone bridge. He lashed the whip toward Roarke, who dodged the spiraling metal tips and spun, swinging his claymore toward Trahern's left leg. The sword struck just below the knee, and putrid blood dribbled from the wound. Trahern growled and lashed again with the whip, striking Roarke just below the temple with one of the metal tips. Gedran groaned, barely conscious. Eislyn dropped her bow and ran to him, dagger drawn to cut him free of his bonds.

As she approached, Trahern turned suddenly and swung his whip, the glowing tips wrapping around Gedran's throat. Regarding Roarke and Gedran dispassionately, Trahern yanked the whip backward. Gedran's neck snapped, the sound echoing in Roarke's mind as he watched his brother's limp body sway from the momentum. Wild magic filled the air, shimmering in the red light. Roarke gasped, his sharp inhale bringing Gedran's magic into his body and bolstering him. Eislyn fell to her knees, a sob ripping from her throat, and Trahern turned to her, a mocking smile on his decrepit face.

He approached her, his whip free and dragging behind

him lazily. "A pity," Trahern said. "I could have had such fun with you under different circumstances."

Roarke roared, pain and anger filling the beastial sound. Power filled him, and his confidence grew as he felt his brother's strength enhancing his abilities. He lunged, slicing his claymore across the back of Trahern's right leg. Trahern shrieked as the metal bit into flesh and sinew. Roarke danced backward, away from his reach. Pain from the slash below his left eye radiated through him. Bloody tears dripped from the wound and congealed in rivulets down his cheek. Trahern struggled to turn toward him, blood flowing freely from the wounds Roarke had inflicted. He slipped in the blood that was pooling at his feet as he turned, falling to his knees before Roarke.

Roarke glanced at Eislyn. The corpses of Trahern's minions lined the ground around them, fallen and filled with Eislyn's arrows before her attempt to free Gedran. She appeared unharmed after their battle, but devastation painted her face. Turning his attention back to Trahern, he swung his sword again, slicing into Trahern's whip arm.

"But you... don't... have... magic," Trahern said between gasps of pain. "You cannot defeat me. You aren't the strongest human."

"The prophecy never said that strength had to do with magic," Roarke said.

"It's true," Eislyn said as she strode to stand behind Roarke. Turning to Roarke, she said, "I finally remembered the phrasing of the prophecy. 'Under a red sun, the strongest man will face the Demon Lord. Driven by what is just and right, only he can bring these shadowed lands back into the light.' It never mentions magic, or where the strength comes from."

"Magic is the only thing that makes you pitiful bags of flesh strong," Trahern said dismissively. He lashed out, deceptively quick despite the injury to his arm, and the whip wrapped around Roarke. Trahern reeled him in like a fish on a line, limiting Roarke's range of motion.

The sword hung useless from Roarke's hands. As he reached Trahern, the Demon Lord reached out with his uninjured arm, grasping the wrapped coils of the whip around Roarke's chest. His long, sharp fingernails scraped across Roarke's skin, rending the flesh below his collarbone. Roarke squirmed, trying to worm away from Trahern.

"You cannot win, boy," Trahern said.

Roarke focused his rage, reaching for the magic he could sense shimmering within him. Dropping his sword, he cupped his right hand. His lips twitched as he mouthed the spell, and a fireball formed in his hand, the flames dancing between his fingers and stretching up the lengths of the whip. It disintegrated into ash, its flakes falling to the ground like snow. Trahern grabbed his arm, pulling him closer still. Smiling, Roarke looked at Trahern and smashed the fireball into his face while he formed a second one in his other hand.

A twang rang out in the air before he could toss it. Trahern abruptly released Roarke, who lost his balance as he stumbled backward. The arrow struck Trahern in the chest. Roarke whipped his head around. Eislyn stood by her horse, bow in hand and a broad smile across her face. Roarke hefted his sword.

"You were saying?" He asked Trahern.

Trahern fell back to his knees and looked up at Roarke. As he opened his mouth to speak, Roarke raised his sword and swung, striking him in the neck and severing Trahern's head from his body. It fell to the ground and the dim red light of the sun began to brighten. Roarke dropped the sword, the weight of battle finally catching up to him, and felt Eislyn's arm come around him. She leaned her head against his upper arm. They stood together, gazing up at the now golden sun.

A loud rumble brought them back to the present. They turned toward Trahern's stronghold and watched as the structure sank. The lava popped and crackled as the stones of the fortress collapsed. Billowing clouds of steam and smoke filled the air around the moat, forcing Roarke and Eislyn to cover their noses and mouths with their arms and run from the ledge. Trahern's body lay prone, his head several yards away, on the edge of the moat. As the rumbling continued, the edges of the ledge gave way and Trahern's head rolled over the edge. With a loud plop, it sank into the lava.

"We did it," Eislyn said quietly. "We actually defeated Demon Lord Trahern."

Roarke leaned his cheek against her hair, nuzzling her. Tears shone in his eyes.

"We did. All three of us," Roarke said. He felt her wrap her other arm around him, enveloping him in a hug.

"I'm so sorry, Roarke."

Roarke leaned into her, resting his forehead against her shoulder and shook as the tears began to flow. "I can still feel him," he sobbed, rubbing his chest over his heart. "Right here. When he died... it's like some of his magic came into me."

Eislyn rubbed his back and held him close. "A part of him will always live on in you."

A short while later, when Roarke's tears had slowed, Eislyn cleaned off his cheek and examined the gash from Trahern's whip.

"You won't need stitches," she said, sounding relieved. "It's a long gash, but it's shallow." She patted his cheek dry, then kissed it gently.

"Another scar." Roarke said.

"I like your scars," Eislyn said, smiling up at Roarke. "Besides, Gedran would probably say that you were too pretty to begin with." She put the rest of the clean cloths back in her pack. "What are we going to do now?"

"Live," Roarke said. "Now, we live."

CHAPTER TWENTY-SIX

Several hours later, Roarke and Eislyn carefully wrapped Gedran's body in Roarke's bedroll. They mounted their horses and took a final look around before they rode away from the wreckage of Trahern's stronghold. Around them, the landscape of the Shadowlands shifted. The strange forest surrounding the stronghold lost its putrid scent. The familiar scent of pine needles and honeysuckle danced on the breeze that floated from the west. The tall stalks of the flowers transformed into sunflowers, and the withered trunks of the dead trees turned into birches and pines. Sunlight shifted between the leaves of the trees, giving everything a golden glow.

"Everything is changing," Eislyn said, her voice filled with awe as she reined in her mount. "With Trahern gone, the Shadowlands are going back to what they once were."

"The trees that grow here look just like the ones in Amadan," Roarke said as he leaned out of his saddle to pluck a morning glory from its vine. He reached over and tucked in behind Eislyn's ear, then caressed her cheek. "I wonder what this place was called before."

"I don't know. I think that knowledge has been lost for a long time. Do you think people will settle here?" Eislyn looked around at the rapidly changing landscape. Grass grew where the rocks and fissures had been before, and wildflowers sprang up in between the larger rocks. She stopped and jumped down from her horse, stretching her legs and picking a few cornflowers. She wove them into the braid that hung along the left side of her neck, the bright colors of the flowers contrasting with her dark hair.

Roarke smiled at her, stunned by the beauty in her simple gesture. He watched as the flowers continued to bloom around them, strengthened by the golden sun and free from Trahern's corruption.

Roarke felt for his stores of magic, pleased to see they were beginning to replenish as the taint left the Shadowlands. He winked at Eislyn, a small flame danced in his palm. She giggled as he twisted the flame's shape, first into an image of himself, then one of her.

"Your magic is working again?" Eislyn asked, excitement filling her voice.

"It seems like it," Roarke said. "I wonder if..." He held up his hands and mimicked the gestures the portal master made the day Gedran was sent to the Shadowlands. A swirl of indigo appeared in the air before them, twisting in on itself rapidly.

Eislyn gasped, staring at the portal. "You can make portals?"

"Seems that way," Roarke said, staring at the portal swirling before them. He focused, and the swirls of indigo faded in the center, a vision of the green pastures behind their cabin appeared.

"Is that..." Eislyn asked.

"Home," Roarke said. "Gedran's and my home, specifically. Quickly, go through. You first, then I'll follow so that I can close the portal."

Eislyn walked her horse through slowly and Roarke followed behind her. The sheep bleated, startled at their sudden appearance in the pasture. They rode through the fields and past the well, pulling their horses up before the cottage. Roarke dismounted, tying his mare's reins to the hitching post just outside the gate. Eislyn stayed in her saddle, watching awkwardly as Roarke turned to her.

"Would you like to come in?" He asked her quietly.

"I would, I should probably go home," she said, her voice trailing off. "We are close enough to the village that someone could see us. It wouldn't be proper for me to be in your home without a chaperone." She looked stricken.

Roarke tried to hide the disappointment from his face. He reached out to her, gently taking her hand. "If we have to follow propriety now that we are back in town, then I hope you will give me permission to call on you," he said.

"Oh yes, of course," she responded. "I would love for you to call on me."

"I suppose this is goodbye, for now," he said. He placed a gentle kiss on the back of her hand. "I will call on you tomorrow."

"I'll wait for you," she said, blushing slightly. She turned her horse toward the town and rode toward the village.

Everything looks exactly the same, he thought. *The pastures are still green, the sheep are grazing... It's almost as though time stopped when I left.* He walked through the front door of the cottage, removing his cloak and hanging it on his hook by the door. The chair by the fire sat where it always had, the leather ottoman their father made in front of it.

"What now?" Roarke asked. "Where do I go from here?" His stomach growled, answering his question.

Roarke walked to the small stove and looked in the cupboards beside it, checking their stores of dried goods. They were well stocked with dried beans and peas, and he had enough oats and flour to last him for some time. He walked back outside and peeked into the root cellar, relieved to see that it still held a large number of potatoes, carrots, beets, and turnips. *I'll need to purchase meat from the butcher in the village, but I have enough vegetables and dried goods to get me through the next few months,* he thought, grabbing a few potatoes and carrots and carrying them inside.

Roarke thought of Gedran as he grabbed the matches and lit the stove, then filled a pot with water. Putting it over the fire in the stove, he began to peel the vegetables, then chopped them into pieces and dropped them into the water to cook. Roarke sat down in the chair opposite the fire and began to clean his sword and belt knife while he waited for the potatoes and carrots to finish boiling. He stared at the empty fireplace, imagining Gedran was with him.

"What do you think will happen to the Shadowlands now?" Gedran asked.

"I don't know," Roarke said. *He reached for his brother and...* He shook himself back to the present, the image of Gedran fading.

"I miss you," Roarke said, looking at Gedran's chair at the little table. "I don't know what I'll do now. Or where I'll go." He took out his journal and pen.

I guess I didn't really think about what would happen if I didn't succeed. The hero always emerges victorious in the stories, and I pictured myself riding back into the village, my brother at my side, triumphant over the evil that had subjugated us for so long. But I'm here, sitting alone beside the cold, dead embers of the last fire he ever lit because I can't bring myself to start one myself. It isn't logical, but I don't want to erase his presence in our house.

I know I'll need a fire eventually. I'll eventually eat the last of the smoked cheese he made, too. But... I'm not ready to be there yet. I'm not ready to say goodbye. I can still feel him here, and his magic is inside me, just beyond the surface. I feel as if I could speak to him through the magic, as though he's really here, somewhere, maybe on a different plane of existence. Maybe I'm crazy. Maybe I'm just grieving for my brother. Maybe it's easier to grieve than it is to figure out what I should do about Eislyn.

What am I going to do about Eislyn? I know nothing of courting and wooing a woman and, even if I did, Eislyn is not your average woman. How do you woo someone who is so much smarter than you? I still can't wrap my mind around what I feel for her. It might be foolish, and it might not work out because we're two very different people who were thrown into an impossible circumstance. Or maybe it will work out. When I call on her tomorrow, assuming her father doesn't kill me on sight, we'll find out, I guess.

Oh Gods, I'll have to meet her father tomorrow.

He stopped writing, wiping the pen clean and setting it between the pages. He rubbed his eyes, his thoughts languid as he stared off into space.

Several hours later, Roarke woke, still sitting in his chair, when the first rays of sunlight shone through the cottage windows. Stiffness wound through the muscles in his neck and back. The fire went out as he slept, and the hearthstones chilled his bare feet. He wrapped the quilt more tightly around himself, gazing out the east-facing window in the back of the cottage. The sun rose over the green pastures, painting the clouds in pastel. He stood, walking into the bedroom and falling into his bed to sleep a bit more.

When he awoke again, he stretched, trying to loosen the knots in his neck and back before walking to the stove and lighting a fire to start breakfast. He let a scraping of butter melt in the pan while he chopped a potato and some onion for a hash. Tossing them into the pan, he ran out to the hen house, hoping the hens had survived to provide him with an egg or two.

"Excellent," he said as he found two eggs nestled in the straw. The last of the hens rustled out to greet him and he tossed some feed toward her as he took the eggs from the nest. "It'll be a good breakfast after all."

He returned to cooking, pushing the hash to one side and cracking the eggs into the pan to cook with a few pieces of dried venison from his pack. He scrambled everything together and tossed it onto a plate and sat down at the table. Gedran's empty chair mocked him, and he felt tears on his cheeks as he stared. *Things will never be the same,* he thought. *No matter what happens next, Gedran will never sit at the table with me and eat breakfast again.*

Roarke took a bite of his eggs and made a face. "It needs salt," he said, shaking his head. "How could I forget the salt?" He added a sprinkle of it to his food, then put it back into the cupboard and returned to the table to eat. He sat quietly, eating the best breakfast he'd had in weeks as a light breeze came through the open windows. The air was warm, and the first signs of summer began to appear in the fields and pastures around them.

The sheep were bleating in the fields when he finished and scraped his plate clean into the trough. He looked at his flock and smiled slightly.

"Well, I guess some things never change," he said to the sheep.

He turned, walking into the bedroom to change into his best jerkin and breeches. He avoided wearing them normally; his mother had spent hours embroidering the edges, and he was loathe to cause any harm to her beautiful handiwork. Dressed, he walked back into the main room and sat down in his chair beside the fireplace. He cleaned his boots, scrubbing the lingering detritus of the Shadowlands from them. When they shined enough that he could almost see his reflection in the scarred leather, he pulled them on and stood.

"What do you think, brother? Do I pass muster?" He asked the empty chair. Gedran's magic flared slightly inside him, lighting the candle on the table for a brief moment. Walking outside, he chuckled as he curried his horse, brushing her mane and tail. Once she was ready, he wandered the pastures, picking wildflowers for Eislyn. He built a bouquet of snowdrops, violets, and vibrant red phlox, finding a few daisies to add to it as he went. He carried the flowers back to the cottage, setting them gently on the table. Heading into the bedroom, he dug out his mother's old sewing basket, searching for one of the ribbons she collected from the peddler whenever she could. He settled on a vivid gold ribbon, carrying it back to the table and wrapping it around the stems before tying it into a bow.

Roarke searched through the old trunk at the foot of Gedran's bed until he found a small leather box buried beneath his parents' treasured possessions. He opened it and gazed at the delicate ring nestled in the center. Set with a small emerald the same color as their mother's eyes, the band was woven to resemble vines and flowers cradling the gemstone. Tears welled in his eyes as he remembered his mother's smile whenever she looked at the ring on her finger.

"Ma," he said, a catch in his voice. "You would have loved Eislyn." He pocketed the box and grabbed the bouquet.

Eislyn's house stood just off the village green, its proud facade tall above the houses surrounding it. He dismounted and tied his horse to the hitching post beside their front walk before striding up the path and knocking on the door. An older gentleman answered the door; Roarke could see the resemblance to Eislyn around his eyes and in the set of his jaw.

"Good day, sir. I've come to call on Eislyn," Roarke said.

"You must be Roarke," the gentleman responded. "We've heard of little else since she returned home from her folly." Hostility brewed below the surface of his polite words.

"I understand that she disappeared without a word. If I had known she was following me, I would have stopped her before she got out of the village," Roarke said. "But I didn't know, and she saved my life more than once. If you'll allow me, I would like to court your daughter."

"After she disappeared with you for weeks, I was hoping you would say that," the gentleman said. "Please come in and sit in the front parlor. I'm Donovan. Let me get her mother so that she can meet you. I'll never hear the end of it, otherwise."

Donovan let Roarke into the house and showed him into the front parlor, which was lined with bookshelves. Large chairs flanked a clay brick fireplace, and a long sofa sat across from the fire. Roarke seated himself on one side of the sofa, careful not to crush the stems of the flowers in his hand from his nervousness. He studied the floor to ceiling bookshelves, admiring the variety of linen and leather covers on the shelves.

It's no wonder she's so brilliant. Look at all these books, he thought. *Didn't she mention that she's read all of the ones in her home?* He stayed seated, but looked around the room, studying the parlor where Eislyn would have spent much of her time. Beside one of the chairs sat a basket of needlework. Brightly colored thread sat atop a piece of white linen, partially worked into a pattern of roses and filigree. Though Eislyn disparaged her own needlework abilities, he could see that her mother possessed exceptional skill. Quiet footsteps in the door behind him caught his attention and he turned his head to look at the door.

Donovan had returned with a lovely woman, clearly still in her prime, who greatly resembled Eislyn.

"Roarke, I'd like you to meet Alana, Eislyn's mother," Donovan said, gesturing to his wife.

"It's a pleasure to meet you, ma'am. Thank you for welcoming me into your home."

"My daughter seems quite taken with you, young man," Alana said, her voice taut. "What are your intentions?"

"My intention is to court and marry her, if she will have me," Roarke said plainly. "During our travels together, she continuously surprised me with her bravery and intelligence. She saved my life more than once, and she gave me hope when I thought I couldn't succeed." His voice broke as he finished, his grief bubbling to the surface. "She kept me going after... after we watched my brother die."

"Why didn't you send her home? You knew that what you were doing was dangerous. You knew it was treason," Alana said, her cheeks reddening as she raised her voice.

"I tried, but she refused to leave me. I don't know why she wanted to help me save my brother, but she was determined to stay, no matter what I said."

"It's true, Mother," Eislyn said from the doorway. "He tried to send me home multiple times, and he constantly put my safety before his."

"Eislyn," Roarke said, standing and holding out the flowers. "These are for you. They reminded me of you braiding the corn flowers into your hair after we defeated the Demon Lord."

"They're beautiful. Thank you so much," she said, eyes shining. A wide smile spread across her face as she sniffed the bouquet. "I'll go put these in water." She left the room to fill a vase, leaving Roarke alone with her parents.

"She said you put her safety before yours. Why would you do that?" Donovan asked Roarke.

"Because she cared enough to help me, even though we didn't know each other well. We had only met once before, at my parents' burial several years ago. She held my hand that day and made me feel like Gedran and I weren't alone." The once-bitter memory now made Roarke smile.

"I remember that day. And to have Gedran selected to go to the Shadowlands... Your family hasn't had much luck," Alana said. "And to lose him... but you still managed to defeat Trahern?"

"Yes. Eislyn's ability with herbs helped me survive a couple of wounds from fighting wyrmlings and gorm, and we found Gedran before the Demon Lord could sacrifice him. Trahern stood between us and Gedran, with his minions charging at our back, and Eislyn was as graceful as the Agrona, her bow singing as she cut down the Gorm with her arrows. She was headed to Gedran to cut him free when... when..." He shifted in his seat, unable to continue as emotions clogged his throat..

Eislyn walked back into the room, carrying a small crystal vase filled with Roarke's flowers. She set it on the mantle, alongside a miniature of her mother, and sat down beside Roarke on the sofa. Alana looked at them steadily from her chair beside the fireplace.

"Mother," Eislyn said, "I know you're angry with me for leaving without a note, but..."

"Eislyn," Donovan said, a warning clear in his voice.

"Please don't hold this against Roarke. He's a wonderful man, a brave man, and I am lucky to have found someone who values me the way he does," Eislyn finished.

"I agree, you are lucky," Alana said, "and I can see how much you care for each other."

"You can?"

"Of course I can. I'm your mother. You look at him the way I look at your father, even after all these years." Alana smiled at Roarke, and he marveled at how much Eislyn resembled her.

"If it would be ok," Roarke said, carefully easing the box from his pocket, "I would like to give this to Eislyn as a symbol of my commitment to her." He blushed and held out the ring box to Eislyn.

She opened the box and gasped, carefully removing the delicate ring. She sprang from her seat and ran to show the ring to her mother.

"Eislyn, will you marry me?" Roarke asked.

"This was your mother's ring," she said, tears filling her eyes.

"It was. She would be thrilled to see it on the hand of the woman I love."

She looked at her parents. Alana wiped a tear from her eye, and Donovan looked on proudly.

"Yes, I'll marry you," she said. She went to sit beside him again, and he grabbed her hand. She handed him the ring and he carefully placed it on her finger, relieved that it fit.

"I have to travel to see the Duke today," Roarke said. "I would like Eislyn to come with me to tell him about what happened."

"I don't suppose that I can say no," Donovan said. "I will come with you, however."

Roarke nodded his acceptance and looked at Eislyn, who sat beside him studying the ring, her eyes misty. He reached out to pat her hand gently.

"We should get going if we want to make it to the Duke's home and back before dark," Roarke said. He stood and held out a hand to help Eislyn to her feet.

"I'll grab a few things and meet you by the hitching post," Donovan said.

Roarke and Eislyn walked out to the hitching post.

"Hello, pretty girl," Eislyn said to Roarke's mare, stroking her mane. The mare nuzzled Eislyn's hand.

Donovan walked around from the back of the house

leading Eislyn's gelding and his stallion. Eislyn grabbed the reins of her horse and climbed into the saddle. Roarke and Donovan quickly followed.

The ride to Duke Laigi's keep passed by without incident. They rode through the rolling hills of Amadan, the dappled sunlight weaving its way through the leaves of the trees along the road. The pastures and fields of Auguistin transitioned to the sprawling buildings of Cahir, the city that surrounded Laigi's keep. As they arrived at their destination, Roarke leapt from his saddle and strode up the stairs where, only a few weeks prior, he and Gedran had been tested. He slammed his fist against the door, knocking loudly. The door creaked open, and an ancient gentleman with stooped shoulders and thinning white hair stood before them.

"Can I help you?" He asked, staring at Roarke and his companions.

"I need to see Duke Laigi. Immediately," Roarke said. "Demon Lord Trahern is dead."

The old man laughed, a startling croaking sound escaping his throat. He quickly succumbed to a hysterical fit of laughter, doubling over and wheezing.

"I'm serious," Roarke said. "I vanquished him."

"But you can't have... The Demon Lord is supposed to be unbeatable."

"Not according to the prophecy. The strongest man could vanquish him. It was never about magic. Only about strength of heart and spirit," Roarke said. "He is gone."

"I will fetch Duke Laigi immediately," the gentleman responded. "Please come in and be seated by the fire."

Roarke helped Eislyn down from her horse, then tied both horses to the hitching post while Donovan took care of his own horse. They entered Laigi's keep and sat beside the fire in the study, waiting for the duke to arrive. Roarke stared at the fireplace and mantle, remembering it from his dream before the testing. He assisted Eislyn, seating her on a small sofa, then sat down beside her. She held his hand, watching the flames dance amongst the old stones of the fireplace and leaned her head against Roarke's shoulder. Donovan hid a small smile at the sight of his daughter's comfort and happiness. He settled deeper into a tufted armchair across from them, stretching his legs out and crossing them at the ankles. At the sound of footsteps entering the room, they all straightened slightly in their seats.

"I understand, from what you told Clyde, that you claim to have vanquished Demon Lord Trahern," Duke Laigi said.

"Yes," Roarke said. "We went in search of my brother, Gedran, and confronted the Demon Lord in his stronghold."

"Preposterous," the duke scoffed. "You're hardly a man, just a boy barely old enough to require a razor. Surely you aren't coming here to confess to treason as a folly?"

"I traveled through the Shadowlands to save my brother and set the duchy on a new path that would no longer require the sacrifice of one of our brothers to keep the peace," Roarke said, standing. "We confronted Trahern at his fortress. We watched him as he snapped my brother's neck with a pull of his whip."

"After Gedran died, there was no other option but to end Trahern and prevent the need for future sacrifices," Eislyn said. "Nothing would have stopped Roarke from avenging his brother."

"Roarke didn't have the magic to pass the testing," Laigi said, an incredulous look on his face.

"That's where everyone was wrong," Roarke said. "It was never about magical ability."

"The prophecy says, 'Under a red sun, the strongest man

will face the Demon Lord. Driven by what is just and right, only he can bring these shadowed lands back into the light,'" Eislyn said, quoting the prophecy to the duke. "It mentions the strongest man, but never states what that strength must be in. It's possible that Caerea didn't know, or chose to omit, where that strength would lie."

"The damned Gods," Laigi blasphemed, staring intently at Eislyn, "and their meddling. Never giving us an easy path to follow. I suppose you must be right, or you wouldn't be here to tell the tale, though I don't know how I can possibly believe you."

"If you require further proof, ride west to the Shadow-lands. They are no longer under a red sun, and the land has become fertile again," Roarke said. "Trahern is gone, and the Shadowlands are no longer. They'll need a new name now."

"I believe they were once called Briomhar," Laigi said. "There are mentions of it in the journals written by my ances-tors from before the treaty was signed."

"Then it should be Briomhar once more," Donovan said. "We should also talk of the reward you plan to give this brave young man."

"And me," Eislyn said.

"And her," Roarke said. "Without Eislyn, I wouldn't have survived."

"I'm assuming that the right to keep their heads isn't the type of reward you're referring to," Laigi said. " Though it would be my right, as they committed treason, no matter the outcome." He shrank back slightly as Donovan glared at him, gripping the arms of the chair. "Do you have any suggestions?"

"Well, for one," Donovan said, "Roarke and Eislyn are newly betrothed. A bridal gift of the land that surrounds Roarke's family home would be a nice start."

Laigi smiled at Donovan, and the negotiations continued.

EPILOGUE

The screams of the baby woke them in the darkest hour of the night. Roarke smiled to himself as he felt Eislyn climb out of the bed beside him and walk across the room.

"Shh," she said quietly to Gedran, "you'll wake Da with all that yelling."

Roarke chuckled quietly, then said, "I'm already awake, my love."

Eislyn brought Gedran into their bed, settling in to nurse him. Roarke stroked the baby's downy hair.

"He's so beautiful," Roarke said, quiet awe filling his voice.

"He looks just like his father," Eislyn responded. She covered Roarke's hand with hers, and they sat together in silence as the baby nursed.

"I wonder if he'll be as strong in magic as my brother was," Roarke said.

"He might be, or maybe he'll prefer a sword like you. Either way, he'll grow up in a world that is safe, and he won't be forced to face a test to determine if he will be sacrificed one day," Eislyn said, a smile in her voice.

"I love you so much." Roarke smiled at her in the dark, then gently caressed her cheek as she fed their son.

"And I love you," Eislyn said. "Moments like this... This is what we fought for."

Staring down at their infant son, nestled in his mother's arms, Roarke knew that Eislyn was right.

ACKNOWLEDGMENTS

A story begins, like many things do, with a dream and the crazy idea that it can be accomplished. I could not have written this story without my amazing editors, Tara Jazdzewski, Seamus King, and Ebony Norwood-Brown, who held my hand through many anxious moments when I believed that I would never be able to do Roarke and Gedran's story justice. Tara believed in me when I didn't believe in myself, choosing to publish my short story, "The Kitchen Witch," in her first anthology, *Of Cottages and Cauldrons*.

To my first babies, Ashly and Ace, thank you for your amazing friendship that inspired Roarke and Gedran, and for your never ending patience when I was writing and frequently forgot everything else as I immersed myself within their world. To my husband, Mikus, thank you for all of the loads of laundry, meals, and surprise cups of coffee, and for being willing to watch sports on TV next to me while I write. There's nobody else in the world who I would rather live this crazy life with, and I am so grateful for every second I get to spend by your side. To Johnny, thank you for being my miracle and giving us the incredible joy you've brought to our lives. I'm so lucky to get to be your mama.

To Skylar, thank you for having my back, listening to me cry and complain, and being so incredibly booksmart that I was able to build Eislyn's intellect around yours. I've known you for most of my life, and each year our friendship gets better and better. Thanks for being my heterolifemate.

To my parents, John and Doris, and my wonderful siblings Jackie, Damion, and Terri, thank you for being the foundation on which my love of words and creativity is built. I am truly the luckiest of women to have such an incredible family, and I am so grateful every day that you are in my corner, encouraging me, and making sure I'm the best I can be. I love you so very, very much.

To Draaven, thank you for reading through my early character sketches and encouraging me to muddy my characters up a bit. You were right. I'm so grateful for your friendship. To Renosh, thank you for putting up with me and not complaining too much when I would write during raid time and forget to dps on trash pulls. I'm glad our paths crossed, and extra glad that you were there to marry Mick and me in World of Warcraft the night he proposed. You're truly the best.

**Book cover artwork by Ruxandra Tudorica |
Methyss Art
www.methyss-art.com**

ABOUT THE AUTHOR

Tiffany Putenis holds a Masters degree in English and Creative Writing from Southern New Hampshire University. Her love for the written word started at an early age, and she continues to be fascinated by works of fiction. Her favorite stories in recent years have been fantasy, but she still has a healthy love of vampires that started in high school when she discovered Bram Stoker and Anne Rice. Tiffany lives in the American Northeast with her husband, three kids, two cats, and a plethora of fish. She loves nature and finds solace in hiking through the beautiful forests that surround her home. You can find her on Twitter (@PutenisWrites), TikTok (@tputeniswrites) and Instagram (@TPutenisWrites).

For updates about Tiffany's writing, visit
www.tiffanyputenis.com

www.ingramcontent.com/pod-product-compliance
Lightning Source LLC
Chambersburg PA
CBHW031021190726

48286CB00003BA/954